Mr E's

MICHAEL EWERS

Mr E's

MICHAEL EWERS

Paul, Hope this kept you
up at night ... in all
the right ways!

CONTENTS

TUESDAYS   1

CIRCLE OF SIX   29

WHAT YOU WISH FOR   41

BLISS   51

CHILD WITH SPIRIT   75

THE TRUTH WILL OUT   117

LIFE'S REPRIEVE   137

REUNION   159

THE DISPLACED   193

TUESDAYS

They say there is a therapeutic value in writing down your thoughts and feelings...your memories. Recording some of the things you've seen and done. But do I dare? I'd have to destroy it as soon as it's written...

It was so many years ago now, yet in my mind I can see it all so clearly. As if the greatest changes in my life had happened just yesterday.

TUESDAY 27th

It seems odd to me now that the most important days of my life, or at least the ones that I remember most, have all seemed to be Tuesdays. The first job that I had, that I liked, I got on a Tuesday. I met my wife on a Tuesday, we got married on a Tuesday and she told me she wanted a divorce on a Tuesday. Best day of my life.

I say that it is odd that Tuesdays have been so good to me, because it was this particular day of the week that I remember disliking so much in the years before. Almost my entire school life I hated

1

Tuesdays. It was always P.E. on a Tuesday afternoon, for years and years I hated that. And later, when I was older, Tuesday morning was a double lesson of chemistry, for two whole years. Legalized torture. Even out of school was hell on a Tuesday: the town would suddenly come under the ownership of shoppers on a Tuesday - market day. No one in their right mind in my hometown would be daft enough to try to go to town on a Tuesday. The place would be overrun by shoppers, farmers and holidaymakers from early in the morning 'til about four in the afternoon. Parking is impossible on a Tuesday. As for getting a Fish 'n Chips... No chance.

Well this particular Tuesday was no different as far as the town was concerned. There seemed to be people everywhere, even on the outskirts of the town, and as usual they were abusing the place. The over-spill car park was nearing full capacity, the football field surface that it served as for the rest of the week, underneath, being completely mangled in the process. Side streets were used for parking, making through traffic have to pass one car at a time and even then with a real danger of losing your wing mirrors. And as for pedestrians, hundreds of them, mostly coming from the direction of the hospital car park that they'd no doubt filled, were everywhere and not one of them seemed to understand that a road is for a car, those big, heavy, moving objects which can maim or kill if you get hit by one. Madness.

I was glad when I got away from it, almost a mile out of the town down a quiet road which led to my house. I can't call it home, it never really felt like my home and on this particular Tuesday it hadn't been my home for a couple of months. I was now confined to the good will of a couple of friends who, luckily for me, had such demanding jobs I hardly ever saw them even though I was living under their roof. The result: we weren't getting in each other's way, yet, and so the arrangement was working.

On the approach to my house I always seemed to form an inward smile, this was Birch Avenue. Twenty-five years ago I'd walk this area and particularly Birch Avenue, with my grandparents and think what it would be like to actually live here. I did for a while. My grandparents would have been real proud. But the prestige of this lovely house in this quiet, ever so slightly upper-class area was never enough to compensate for the witch of a wife I had to endure life with.

Strangely, stopping the car was an effort, I so wanted to just drive on by but I stopped, paused, gathering a few errant thoughts about what to say if she was in a good mood and what I should try not to say if she was in a bad mood, and then opened the car door.

December was just a few days away and I can remember the cold hitting me as I opened that door. Strange how little things like that stick in your mind. As usual the road and paths were clear, even of leaves, except maybe the stray one or two. This area of the town always received good attention from the services. Money talks I suppose, but more likely the new currency, who you know rather than how much you have.

The drive gates were open, but no way was I

going to drive up to the door. In one of her bad moods in times gone by she'd thrown a flowerpot which smashed my windscreen and badly dented my bonnet. Now with a new car, something else I wanted to keep away from her, I was taking no chances.

The lawn needed mowing, even if it was late November. The borders didn't look as if they'd been tended to for too long and surprise surprise the trees hadn't been cut back, but then she always hated my trees.

Still a few steps away from the front door I could hear the television, she always liked it loud enough for the neighbours to know what she liked to watch. She would have them believe that she watched the arty channels, opera and documentaries on art and the like. In truth she would leave the television blaring away and go upstairs to watch cheap and tacky quiz shows, trying in vain to get two consecutive answers right.

I rang the bell and waited: waiting to be asked to enter my own house.

The door opened slowly, I knew immediately that she wasn't opening it, it must be Cal, now five and certainly not old enough to opening the front door to god knows who.

"How's my big boy?" I said as I saw him or words to that effect anyway. I always regarded myself as not very good with kids I didn't know and prided myself at being very good with my own son. But now, after just a few months of hardly seeing him he seemed like someone else's child. To my shame I felt uneasy around him and struggled to find the right words whenever I tried to speak to him. Using the telephone was agony.

"Dad," he shouted. He leapt forward and grabbed my leg, gave it a hug and then ran off in to the house announcing to whoever was home that I had arrived. Not necessarily the best way to make a discreet visit.

And then there she was. Angela. She was in the lounge doorway, make up applied as if with a trowel. I'm not sure, but I think I actually smelt her before I saw her. 'Nature's Poison' was her chosen fragrance, had been for years. She squirted it on every couple of hours and left a trail of overpowering fragrance everywhere she went, hell when we were first together she'd squirt a few sprays in to her bath water before getting in. I hated the stink then, and it grew more nauseating as time went by. Now, I think I was desensitizing to it a bit, I didn't gag on the spot.

I could tell by the look on her face and stance that she was well hung over. "Jason. Aren't you supposed to call before you come over?" she asked, eyebrows raised painfully high.

"You called me. Last night?"

She didn't seem to know what I was talking about. "Half past midnight...? Ring any bells...?"

"Oh, well you'd better come in then," she said still not seemingly aware that she'd called me at all.

I closed the front door and followed her in to the lounge where the television still blared. "Hello Jason," a familiar voice said before I'd cleared the doorway.

"Pam," I said acknowledging my old next-door neighbour with whom I'd always gotten along very well. Angela had always tried to give the impression she liked Pam but behind closed doors she hated her for her genuine superiority in pretty much every field. "How are you keeping? It's been a few months."

"I'm very well, thank you Jason. And you are looking good, if I may say so," she smiled and got to her feet. "We can finish this later Angela if you like," she gestured to the television.

"No it's alright," Angela stopped the video playback, silencing the room. "Jason won't be long, then we can get back in to it." She turned to me, "You understand we are in the middle of something and don't want to lose track."

"Of course," I said not being able to restrain myself, "Puccini?"

Angela nodded, "Madam Butterfly," she sounded so sure of herself that I just knew I had to add something.

"I like some of his work, but it never fails to amaze me that someone in that day and age could have succeeded in writing something as beautiful as that in spite of his disability."

Angela didn't flinch, "There have been many a disabled genius."

Pam was looking at me, already aware of what I was doing. She knew my little moments of fun at Angela's expense of old. She was obviously suppressing a smirk.

"But still, writing music while virtually stone deaf. It just strikes me as amazing. True genius, I can't imagine how he'd have even started."

"I'm going to check on Cal, and give you some privacy," Pam was off and I just knew she'd be laughing as soon as she was out of earshot.

There was a moment of silence. I thought about sitting down even though she hadn't offered but thought better of it. If I stayed standing I could make a quicker departure. "So do you remember calling me last night?"

"Yes, of course I remember," which meant that she didn't but wouldn't admit it. "I'm just not sure what it was about."

It was time to play the nice guy so I decided to throw her a lifeline, "Mind if I go see Cal for a couple of minutes? Maybe you'll remember if you think of it for a while?"

She waved her hands as if dismissing me so I took that as a yes. I hadn't even taken one step before my mind started lining up things to say to Cal.

He was out back in the house extension, which housed a small swimming pool. I was grateful that Angela had had the brains to cover the pool for safety even though I'd made sure from as early as possible that Cal was a good swimmer. Pam was kneeling by him and together they were filling little lorries with sand and pebbles and trailing them around a plastic sand box. "Having fun there?" I asked. Original I know.

"Dad. Can you stay and play? Please."

How do you say no to a child? Big bright eyes, a smile on his face and all the innocence I've lost. "Only a couple of minutes. I'm sorry."

He didn't seem to take it too bad, I couldn't exactly say 'I can't stop because I'd like to throttle your mother and she'd like me out of the way as soon as possible so I don't see her next toy boy arrive'.

"Why don't you show your dad what the blue truck does?" Pam suggested as she got to her feet. "I'm so sorry about Puccini's ears. Shaving accident was it?"

"I don't know how you do it," I told her.

"Taking regular doses of," she nodded to the house so as not to say Angela's name in front of Cal, "constantly feigning interest and knowledge in something she hates, is one of the few enjoyments left to me. She hates having to sit through these things. And I've ordered a four and a half hour version of Hamlet. It'll cripple her." she walked off smiling.

I turned my attention back to Cal.

My wonderful son showed me a large pick-up truck, fairly new, that had three white buttons on the side. Each one made different sounds and made lights flash. He thought it was one of the best things he'd ever seen.

We had a good few minutes, I even managed to have a few short conversations with him. How he was, how he liked school, was he chasing any girls at break time, that sort of thing. It was the best five or so minutes I'd had with him in over three months and it came to an end too soon for me.

"Jase." I hated the way that woman would shout for me and even more so that she would call me 'Jase'.

"Coming," I called back and then said my goodbyes to Cal.

Angela returned to playing duty as I got up, "He is doing good Jason," she told me, seriously.

"I can see."

"Did you tell your Dad about your scout trip

Cal?" she asked him.

"What's this?"

He told me that next Monday he was going to spend the night camping out with his scout group and I could tell that he was so excited about it that he couldn't believe that he'd forgotten to tell me.

"Are you old enough for that?" I asked it as a joke but meant it quite seriously. Angela explained that it was an orientation exercise to see how he'd cope with being away from home. There'd only be about half a dozen boys going and several adults. She seemed to think it was okay, which allayed my fears a bit, I wasn't about to ask Angela for the details, that might let her in on my best kept secret. That I cared.

*

She had obviously had a drink.

I scanned the room quickly for evidence of a glass or the wet ring on the table, she never used a coaster, but saw nothing.

"I'm concerned that Cal might be affected by our splitting up," she announced. My God it almost sounded as if she cared.

"A few months after announcing that you want a divorce is a little late to be thinking that. Don't you think?"

"You hear so much these days about children growing up confused, getting in to trouble. They mix with the wrong people. You see it on the television all the time..." She paused, I suspected for dramatic effect. Softly she added, "It might be easier if you took a step back a bit."

"I beg your pardon?" When I get angry I always get polite, so I'm told.

"I was thinking that it might be better for Cal if I asked for sole custody. Of course we would arrange for you to see him, but perhaps in time he would think of you more as an uncle than a father. After all, we are going to meet other people, eventually."

I think I heard all that she was saying, but it was difficult to tell, as by now I was experiencing a strange buzzing in my head. There was a definite adrenalin rush and anger by the truck load, but that's probably what she wanted. If she could make me angry, especially with a witness nearby. I thought of the innocent Pam out back, not to mention Cal himself, if she could cause a scene then she'd have a case for the sole custody.

I don't think I was speechless for long, but she had to ask me what I thought.

"I think something like that has some sense to it, but I need time to get my head around it." At times of confusion, waffle and stall.

I was suddenly aware that I had sand under my finger nails, perhaps because my fists had been clenched. "Can I go and wash my hands? I'm a bit sandy."

"Of course Jase. Use the kitchen, there's some new liquid soap in there that smells really..." I was out of ear shot.

'Use the kitchen' indeed. What was that supposed to mean? There was a down stairs loo, but well, what the hell. She does think it's her house.

From the kitchen sink window, I couldn't quite

see in to the 'pool-house', as Angela liked to call it, to where Cal was playing. I almost moved across to the far end of the kitchen so that I could see him, but why should I put myself through that right now? She already had me worked up and... Arh, yes of course, that would be her twisted little way. That was why she directed me to the kitchen, so I'd be tempted to see how happy Cal was. Happy without me. Perhaps I'd feel so sorry for the little guy that I'd say yes to her plan. A little tug at the heartstrings?

I said she was a devious witch.

TUESDAY 4th

Tuesday morning. The sun is out, there's a slight frost and as I step out of the house there's little noise, no birds, a quietly running engine somewhere near....well, there was an engine.

It's early. Colin and Marie, the friends I'm living with were out late last night so won't be up for a while so it's time for me to have a little q.t., that's quality time. Angela always called it q.t. for some reason, a habit I suppose I've picked up. My latest form of quality time with just myself is a fifteen minute jog, just long enough to completely knacker me out, followed by long hot soak in a bath. Two things that Angela hated. She always laughed at the idea of my jogging, probably because any attempt she might make at it would only serve to give her two black eyes. As for a long hot soak, in her mind, there's only one person allowed that luxury and that was Angela. Well things have changed now.

I had just about managed, maybe twenty steps,

not enough to get any sort of rhythm when I exited the drive straight in to two men, almost knocking one of them to the floor, "Oh, I'm sorry. Excuse, me. I should've looked before shooting out," I was trying to apologize... I didn't even notice that the guy I was helping to his feet was a uniformed Police Officer.

"No harm done," was the curt response, no pleasantries these days. Not from police anyway.

"Well, all the same..." then I noticed the uniform.

The expression on my face must have said it all. The penny dropping in my head could almost have been audible. "Can I help you? I live just here, for now anyway."

"This is the address we've been given for a Mr Jason Ryan. Would that be you sir?" The other guy had asked me this, I'd barely noticed him after realising that I'd just ran in to a policeman. "Sir. Could you tell me where I can find Jason Ryan?"

"I'm... I am Jason Ryan," I said, the words seemed to come out in slow motion.

"Could we have a word inside sir?"

Suddenly my world was heaving back and forth, my legs felt like jelly, then when I tried to move they seemed more like lead. "Is something wrong? Not Cal?"

"Please sir, if we could just speak inside." The other man, obviously a police officer too was in plain clothes, a poorly cut suit but fancy tie. I guessed he picked his own suits and his wife picked his ties. "This way sir?" he asked, I was reassessing the tie wondering if being silk he had a 'partner' rather than a wife. It was a very nice tie.

Men don't usually have such good taste when it comes to ties. Not the marrying sort anyway.

"Uhmm, yes, sure. We can go in..." I lead them, a little dazed.

We didn't speak until we were in the kitchen, I was quick to take a seat, my legs thanked me in some kind of internal language only your body really understands, but I got the message.

"May I?" the plain-clothes officer asked. He sat, the uniformed one pulled a chair out a little way from the table and also sat.

"Cal?" I asked again.

"I'm Inspector Tailor," he showed me a piece of paper in a holder, no shiny badge like you see in the American movies.

"Cal is your son?"

"Yes."

"Your son is nothing to do with why we're here. A Miss Pamela Henderson has told us that he's away on a scout trip. Is that right?"

I paused, "Yes, that's right. At least as far as I know."

"Mr Ryan, a little over an hour ago Miss Henderson discovered the body of your wife in her kitchen."

"Body?"

"Yes."

"As in... As in dead?"

"I'm afraid so sir. Miss Henderson has already made a positive identification, it seems as though she died by a blow to the back of the head."

I let things hang for a moment, this was like nothing I've ever experienced before.

"You understand that my wife and I are..."

another pause, "...were, in the process of getting a divorce."

"Miss Henderson did explain that you were separated."

"So what do I have to do now?"

"At this time sir, make yourself available to us. There's nothing else to be done until we know exactly what happened at that house last night."

The police officers got to their feet, "You weren't with your wife at all last night sir?"

"No. I was here last night."

"What's going on?" Marie had arrived at the kitchen door without anyone noticing.

"I think," I got to my feet. I had tears in my eyes and needed space. "I really, really, need that run now..." I was out of the kitchen and running, not jogging, but running. It seemed to do the trick for a while.

*

Colin and Marie tried everything they could to make me feel better. There was freshly ground coffee brewing when I got back and Colin had run a hot bath.

I didn't need any of it, I was just glad that the police were gone and that things were, in appearance quite calm.

I really wanted to go and get Cal.

How do you talk to a child? Now it's what do you say to a child?

I was on the top of the stairs, I found myself just being there for a while. There's a full-length mirror there and for some reason I always found myself paused in front of it. Now I knew I'd been there for a few minutes and on some level I was hearing the conversation between Colin and Marie, but I wasn't registering it properly.

Colin said that perhaps her latest boyfriend had smacked her one. We all knew how mouthy she could get after she'd had a few drinks, maybe she brought it on herself. He mentioned how she'd spoken and acted towards Jason.

Marie was more inclined to think it was the drink. She liked her drink and had taken many a fall under the influence. Perhaps this time she fell on a hard floor and did some damage.

Both theories were good, I remember thinking that both theories were good. But then theories tend to be. But theories are just that, theories.

They stopped talking as I started down the stairs, they could obviously hear me coming.

Marie forced a hot over-sweet cup of coffee into my hand.

"I want to go and get Cal, but I'm not sure that I should drive right now," I said. I was about to ask Colin, but he offered.

"I'll take you mate. No problem."

"Thanks. Marie, could you get in touch with them, let them know I'm coming and why? Please?"

She hugged me. She was never a touchy feely kind of person, other than with Colin of course. She hugged me and kissed me on the cheek, her husband was stood at my side I didn't know where to look. "I'll see to it. And you give that little man a hug from me." She hugged me again.

Isn't it amazing how a shock to your system can make you act in a totally different way?

*

The trip wasn't a long one, not surprisingly the scouts hadn't gone far for their first overnight stay away.

Colin and I talked briefly on the way, he asked me what I'd tell Cal. I said that I'd have to come up with something that wasn't an outright lie. I couldn't lie to the lad, but there's no way I could tell him that she was lying dead on the floor in his home.

He told me about what Marie had said about the drinking. I didn't like to say that I'd overheard them. Perhaps that was something that Cal might be able to understand, he'd seen his mother drunk far too many times. He knew that drinking makes people fall over - well in a child's mind that could be how it seems.

I broke the silence a few miles later by telling him that I'd seen her just yesterday. I'd spent a week going mad looking for a ring I'd had off my father, just a plain ring with a tiny emblem that was almost worn away. I thought the only place it could be was in Angela's kitchen, that maybe I'd taken it off when I'd washed my hands there last Tuesday. I told him that at about one fifteen, I know the time 'cause I was on my lunch break, she'd already had a few drinks and was a little loud. If she'd carried on for a few more hours she'd have been in quite a state.

Colin didn't say anything.

*

For a five year old my little man really surprised me. He knew something was wrong even before I'd arrived. When it was me that drove up he knew it must be about his mother. I don't think even I would have made that connection so quickly at my age.

We sat by a brook for about ten minutes talking.

I told him that his mother had fallen over, explained that sometimes, if you fall backwards you can bang your head and that can be very serious. I told him, without too much window dressing, that his mother had hurt her head very badly and was no longer with us. He knew about heaven, I haven't got a clue how, I'd never believe that Angela could have approached that subject with him.

Was she in Heaven? Like Hell was she.

But at this point I did lie. Yes, the wicked witch of Birch Avenue was in Heaven and she'd be waiting there for us. Perish the thought. The idea made me shudder.

We sat in silence for a while, then walked slowly to Colin's jeep. I thanked the Scoutmaster for looking after Cal. He said he'd have Cal's stuff forwarded in a few days. We left.

Tuesday 11th

The police concluded that there was no foul play at work in the matter of the death of Angela Ryan. She had a huge amount of alcohol in her system, more than enough to make it difficult for her to walk, but she could take her drink, I knew better than that.

The kitchen floor had been slightly wet, it would have been more so the night before. It seems she was trying to transfer mineral water from a bottle in to a jug and had spilt it. Being unsteady on her feet she'd slipped and as she fell, her back now to the sink, she hit her head on the edge of the worktop.

Somehow they made it all sound so simple.

But as I stood there, alone at her graveside I knew that the simple story that the world knew was just that.

A simple story.

Present Day

Well, there you have it. And yes after unloading like that I do feel a lot better. I think that actually means that a shrink has done something right for me after all this time.

So, now you want to know just what did happen on the night of Monday 1st of December?

That's complicated, kind of. In my mind it's clear as day, but events moved so quickly that night and in the days that followed.

I've realised as I've been writing this that I did make a mistake. They say people like me always do. Well, thankfully the Police weren't around to hear it. By the brook, I told Cal how his mother died. No one had told me at that point. Good job Marie had made the suggestion as a possible means of her death. Good job Colin was out of earshot, he's clever enough to have maybe put two and two together. Doubt if he'd have said anything though.

The simple facts are that I went to see her at lunchtime. She was drunk and loud. She was pissed off that Pam had gone away to see her sister for the day and so she couldn't even call on her for company. In truth it was more likely that her boyfriend had stood her up, hardly surprising when I think back to how she was that day. Who knows, maybe he walked out on her because she was drunk.

She started telling me about her plans for the future. Living the single free life for a few years, travelling a bit, seeing the world. Then she'd settle down, find herself a nice wealthy guy who looked as if he only had a few years left in him. The woman made me feel sick to my stomach.

And what about Cal?

"What about him?" That's what she said.

Suddenly everything just fell in to place, as if I wasn't even in control of my own body.

While she was at the freezer getting ice I picked up the spare back door key from where it had hung since we had first moved in. I doubt whether that key had even been used until the night I used it.

As she was leaving the kitchen I purposely dropped my keys by the power points to the side of the fridge and as I leaned down I checked she wasn't looking. I switched off the plug to the rear security light.

I headed back to work getting a spare key to the back door cut on the way. When I got back to work I didn't give another thought about what I would do later, I just knew I'd figure it out without having to worry over details then and there.

In the evening Colin and Marie were getting ready to go out, I sat down in front of the television ready for a movie marathon. I had a huge bag of popcorn, two of my favourite videos 'Fight Club' and 'Star Wars' on video to watch and a bottle of wine to add the final touch.

I remember Colin asking whether I had everything that I wanted as I rearranged his furniture so that I was in a big arm chair just a few feet back from the TV.

They were out by eight, I got things moving. I forwarded the 'Star Wars' tape to the end so it would look as if I'd watched it, and forwarded about half way through the 'Fight Club' tape ready for when I got back. I swilled half the wine down the sink and emptied most of the popcorn in to a carrier to dispose of en route. There's no way I could eat all that stuff before or after what I had to do tonight.

I changed my clothes. I felt really stupid wearing black everything, but well, what the hell... At least I kind of looked the part, and wouldn't be immediately recognized even by someone who knew me. Black has never been my colour. I thought about my shoes, it might be a good idea to wear the ones I'd worn earlier, but no, I opted for old trainers which I could ditch on the way home, I picked up some new ones to change in to on the way back. Oh and gloves, I almost forgot gloves, thick padded ones, hopefully they'd not only prevent finger prints but also deceive my hand size, in the event of any trouble later. Well you never know.

It was a good half an hour walk, I didn't want to risk anyone noticing that I'd driven off. A car, even a fairly new one would make a noise easily noticed in a quiet area late at night. I gave myself plenty of time, I was out of the house by nine thirty.

I dumped the popcorn into a wheelie bin a few houses away, then placed my new trainers inside another bin a bit further on.

I was stood at the front of her house, my bloody house, by ten fifteen. Had the security light been switched back on? No. Good. I moved around back and waited.

I watched her saunter through the house like some kind of lady, which she wasn't, for over an hour. She drank, sang a bit, argued with the television and then the telephone rang. I suddenly realised that this was my chance to open the door and step inside.

As the phone rang and she took her time to answer it, as always she did. I took advantage of the noise, moving only as the ringer sounded. I was inside, the door closed and hiding in the kitchen before she shouted her abusive hello to the caller.

She argued for ages. I was glad of that because it gave me the chance to warm up a bit, I was near frozen. The language coming from the lounge was unbelievable, even for her, and I'd lived with her for almost six years. Believe me she could swear with the best of them. Then the phone seemed to get slammed down, or thrown and there was silence.

I could hear her moving around then I heard her shout, "Damn it!" and it sounded as if a bottle got thrown and smashed. Then I heard the clip clop of her heels on the tiled hallway.

She was coming.

I was stood to the side of the doorway as she entered, oblivious to my presence. She put the light on, I cursed under my breath. She went to the fridge and pulled out a bottle of the posh water she always liked, the one in the fancy blue bottle. Disgusting stuff, I'm sure she only drank it because it was the 'posh' variety. For some reason she always liked it to be in a decanter, like the rest of her drinks, so went to the sink and tried to transfer it.

I stepped slowly up behind her.

My arms went out, I used so little pressure it was amazing. I surprised myself. Her head went up, I spun her round. The bottle fell in to the sink and the decanter smashed to the floor.

Her legs went out from under her. She was so weak, perhaps surprised, perhaps drink, she was like a rag doll. I jerked her back and downward, cracking her head on to the work top surface. I knew I had to apply a good hard force but couldn't risk pressing her skin hard enough to bruise her. Would this have been enough?

The cracking sound of her head on the work top edge said it all. I was sure the job was done. I looked her straight in the eye, the last thing she saw as the life in them seemed to just go out. It only took a second or so and she was limp. I let her go.

She slid a little on her way to the floor; I wasn't in the slightest bit phased by the blood trail down the unit door. I just took a moment and then concentrated on the 'scene'.

Firstly I put the old spare door key back on the hook where it was supposed to be. I'd be able to lock the back door on my way out with the key I'd had cut. 'No signs of forced entry'.

I picked up the bottle of water that had fallen in the sink, lifted her legs up and dropped it on the floor from about waist height. It smashed, water and blue glass spread out, then I put her legs back down. 'The bottle of water smashed to the floor before she died'.

Taking care not to step in the water I took off her shoes, lifted the torso a little and scratched them in to the floor. 'She must have slipped with her high heels on the wet floor'.

I took her pulse.

I couldn't believe it. The bitch was breathing. Faint, but she might actually survive.

I closed her mouth with one hand and pinched her nose with the other. She soon stopped breathing.

The security light had to be switched back on or else that would look suspicious. I looked over to Pam's house, all her lights were out, she was probably in the front of the house or maybe in bed. It would probably be an acceptable risk to take. I switched it back on at the plug.

I stood up and checked everything out. It looked okay I thought and I left, quickly and quietly. The security light didn't come on until I was half way through my escape.

Almost home I had to concentrate to remember the bin I'd put my trainers in. I collected them and ducked in to a garden to change unspotted by any traffic that might pass. Someone changing shoes on the side of the road late at night would be something a person would remember if there were an investigation by the Police. The old ones were pulled off in seconds, but the new ones had to remain looking new, Colin or Marie would notice if they were suddenly mud-soaked. I took my time putting them on, tied them properly and made sure not to walk through the flowerbed as I had on my way into the garden.

I got home, changed my clothes - which I would destroy in the next day or so - and settled down to the second half of 'Fight Club'. As I pressed the play button on the machine I noticed the time, it was just past midnight. Yes. Another Tuesday. Another fabulous Tuesday.

I downed a full glass of wine and started rubbing my eyes, I turned the light off and waited for Colin and Marie to return.

When they did, I was looking tired. The lights they switched on dazzled my eyes and the film was almost finished.

"Had a good night?" they each asked. Colin leaned over and picked up the wine bottle, nearly empty now. "I should say he has."

The term 'Hook, Line and Sinker' comes to mind, now just as it did back then.

I knew it was only a matter of time before the Police confronted me and as it happened I was genuinely surprised when I did 'bump' in to them. I remembered to jump to the conclusion that it must be about Cal they were coming to see me about and played the rest by ear. Eyes wide, tears welling, shaking by the very real fear of discovery, the performance as it happens fooled everyone. There never was any investigation, within hours they were saying accident and that was pretty much it.

I have visited her grave a few times. I make a

point of telling her how much happier everyone is now. Now that she's dead. I even took flowers on a couple of occasions, for appearances.

Cal, my wonderful son has grown up in to a fine young man of whom I am extremely proud. He doesn't speak of his mother very often and I do try not to blacken his mind towards her. His memories of her drunken rages do that all by themselves.

Pam is gone now. She had a lingering illness, which claimed her a few years ago. I'm proud to say that I helped to better her quality of life somewhat with the best medical help and round the clock nursing, thanks in part to Angela. It seems the inept police helped me, quite unwittingly, claim against a very substantial insurance policy. I was sure that greedy cow would have cashed it in, but apparently not. Thank God for the modern police force, hey?

Any regrets, you ask?

Just one.

I regret that it was Pam who found the body. I'd hoped it would have been found by one of her toy boys. That would have been a hard one to explain. Having his way with a married woman nearing her forties with a five year old child in the house - no self-respecting gigolo would want that sort of attention. On the other hand maybe in their world it would have been good for business.

Was it worth it?

Absolutely.

When her head went thud and the light of life in her eyes went out, I saw my freedom. Freedom in her eyes and fulfilment in my heart. I just wish I'd done it sooner... I suppose, perhaps in some

ways, that too might qualify as a regret?
　　Would I do it again?
　　Already have.

CIRCLE OF SIX

Stone Gate Cottage is a normal kind of cottage by most people's standards. The cottage is nothing special to look at and there is nothing worthy of any great degree of remark within it either. Fittingly there have never been any occupants that have given the place any 'character' and no visitors distinguished enough to be worthy of mention.

I visit this particular cottage from time to time and do so with a certain very select group of people. I suppose one might loosely call them friends, but they aren't people I usually mix with other than when I visit the cottage.

There are six of us in all: I first came to this place at the age of 27. One might say I was in the prime of my life, others might be justified in calling me an over-eager whipper-snapper and, trust me, quite a few did indeed say just that... there were one or two who went a great deal further.

There's no point in me going to any great detail about myself, or any of the others really, so I shall be brief. My main pastime would have been enjoying life, quote unquote, if you know what I mean. I would work at a job that required virtually no mental ability just to have enough money in my pocket at the end of the week to enable me to join my friends for the obligatory Friday and Saturday night piss-ups: an occasion that was more than it might seem to the untrained observer. I, indeed we, my friends and I, used to know how to enjoy ourselves. The Friday night would start at about seven o'clock (not by choice, that was forced on us by our working hours) with a drink at each house we would visit as we walked from the outskirts of town, picking up our friends one by one. Only one of my friends lived further out of the centre of town than I did so the two of us would have had more to drink than the others by the time we got to the last guy's house. We'd hit the bars at around eight and with a mixture of drinking, dancing, drinking, flirting, drinking, fighting and drinking we would be ready for the obligatory take-away by about mid-night. This was the 'silly-hour'. It was as if somehow God had decided that any single guy out for a drink would lose control of his legs when the clock struck twelve. Anyway, we would have great fun on Friday night, maybe topped off with a slanging match of some kind on the way home and if it was a good night we'd even have a mass vomiting session on someone's lawn...no one we knew of course...

Saturdays would have a slightly different formula because Saturday nights were 'pulling' nights. On Saturdays my mates would meet up with the girls they'd chatted up on the Friday night – a bullet I would have to carefully dodge. My idea of a date wouldn't exactly go down well with my mates. As people would pair off I'd become free to start chatting up someone more to my taste without the worry of being spotted. Whatever we got up to we knew we would all soon be exchanging stories of what we got up to – of course as I told my story I'd have to change the gender of my 'partner'. A small price to pay for being able to have a social life. You'd be amazed at the things we'd get people to do under the influence of drink that they would never agree to when sober. Wow! I still can't help but smile at the things I got up to and the places too...

Suffice to say that I would have been referred to perhaps as a 'lad'... Not a bad thing to be called, I know of many people who've been called worse.

Now, to get back to the cottage, the other people who join me there are a sedate bunch, perhaps a rather sober bunch, but while I wait for them I suppose I could tell you a little bit about them...

Oh, my name's Graham by the way, I suppose I should have mentioned that earlier.

As I was saying, the others who visit the cottage with me are the quiet sort, three other guys and two women. The guys are Jim, Marshall and Daryn. The women are Renee and Jaqueline.

Jim is the teacher type. He did some teaching many years ago and now seems to think that everyone is his pupil, that's certainly how it seems from the way he talks to people. Underneath he's a caring, heart-in-the-right-place kind of guy.

Marshall strikes as the sort of guy whose brain was put in backwards, I don't mean that in a horrible way, it's just that he's a bit slow on the uptake sometimes.

Daryn's a mere teenager and prone to speaking before realising what it is he's saying. Over time I think he's become so self-conscious, it is getting increasingly difficult to get him to say anything.

Anyway, Renee: she's a bit older than the rest of us. Kind of the mother figure of the group. She tends towards a raised voice, even when she's just having a normal conversation - not that I've ever had a normal conversation with her... But then I suppose I've never had what you'd call a 'normal' conversation with any of them. Conversation never seems to happen at the cottage, it's almost like an unwritten rule.

Finally, Jaqueline: she's only a year or so older than me and we seem to get on quite well. My overriding impression of her is that she's very tall. Isn't it strange how you can see someone and think they're tall and yet you see someone else of the same height and their height doesn't even register?

Of course there's probably lots more to tell, but I don't see the point, we don't talk much so don't know much of any interest. Our little get together only lasts for like, half an hour or so and let's face it, you aren't going to get to know people that well in the occasional half hour here, half hour there. In addition to that, the experiences at the cottage have so profoundly challenged and I suppose changed all of us that none of us are really like ourselves anymore... Well, not when we're at the cottage anyway.

I can't believe that it's me once again who gets to pace around this damn place on his own waiting for the rest of them. Why am I always the one left wandering around endlessly?

Same dingy room.

We always use the same room.

I think the cottage in previous years had a very big family in it. It seems to have that feel. Like as if the house is now relaxing after having been bursting at the seams with the hustle and bustle of a big and very loud family. Funny how buildings give off vibes like that.

"You're here first again."

That's the unmistakable voice of Renee.

"Yes, it seems to be the way of things," I reply. I could of course comment on how everyone else is so tardy. Time and time again, so tardy, but best not ruffle feathers unnecessarily, especially so early in the evening.

"Well Jim and Daryn are right behind me, so brace yourself."

"Do we know what bee is in Jims' bonnet tonight?" I ask, not caring, for it is sure to be complete nonsense. I do feel so sorry for Daryn, he's so young and he seems to feel obliged to just take the verbal explosion that Jim is likely to enter into if allowed. I suppose there is indeed some degree of innocence in youth after all. Maybe that's why Jim usually seeks Daryn out, he knows he won't tell him to shove a brick in his talking hole.

And there we have it... Jim's voice clearly audible. And I have just a matter of seconds left before he descends, in all his glory.

"Brace yourself," Renee said, a sly glint in her eye.

The conversation, well, more of a monologue

really, became understandable seconds later. I looked at Renee in sheer disbelief; I couldn't believe the degree of passion with which Jim was discussing the number of teats on the udders of cows.

As they entered, poor Daryn looked almost zombified by the conversation. His face lit up with the prospect of other company while Jim was silenced...perhaps from the fear of being told he was talking something else, which we refer to as of the cow...or of the bull...

"Well I see we are gathering already," Jim said in that jovial head-teacher type of way, the sort of thing where they wring their hands a little and smile as if troubled with constipation but don't want anyone to know.

"Now how about we take our seats so that when the last two get here we can get started as soon as possible. I have a good feeling about tonight. Energized. That's the word. I feel energized at the thought of tonight, I'm sure it's going to be a good one."

Renee had her head down, she was already seated at the table and was trying to clear her mind, she was into meditation in a big way, but I suppose she needed to be. Daryn and I exchanged a glance as Jim noisily dragged a chair over to the table and sat himself down next to Renee. I felt sorry for her, but it was a half-hearted sort of sorrow because at the same time I was so thankful that Jim hadn't decided to try to sit next to me. We were none of us great conversationalists, our situation dictates that but we did sometimes make the effort. It was Jim's conversation we all dreaded. We were all aware of how much effort he put into it, yet at the same time he was almost always talking the stuff of cesspools.

Marshall's arrival moments later was an understated affair. He entered, there were a few glances and that was that. He knew he had to be there and he knew where 'there' was. That was enough for Marshall.

With his arrival and his immediate move to seat himself to the other side of Renee I thought it best to take up my seat and gestured Daryn to do the same. We were just one short, but by the time we were seated, Jaqueline too was entering. No words were spoken, she saw us, pulled a seat to the table and completed the six.

I suppose to the outside observer we would appear an odd bunch but here we sat... Yet again! Sitting on dusty old chairs around a dusty old table, waiting for Renee to signal that we were ready to start our little ritual. A ritual that we now went through six times every year.

Renee, being the oldest and perhaps the clearest of mind, was the one who took control now. She took a deep breath, her chest filled noticeably and opened her eyes wider than I thought was healthy, "I think we can begin," she announced.

All six of us took our cue and started to hold hands in a circle around the table.

It was frowned on for anyone to speak from here on unless spoken to, so the room filled with a silence which we'd all heard so many times before. It was a unique silence, one of exhilaration, expectation and excitement and yet tainted with profound sadness and, for most of us, worry.

After a few minutes of silent concentration and channelling Renee broke the circle. "It is no good. I can't get through to anything at all," she complained.

"We still have time left," Jim announced. He looked towards the rest of the group, "We must concentrate harder, picture those we wish to contact." He looked back to Renee, "You will try again, won't you?"

After a glance at the rest of us, Renee conceded with a weary nod. She took Jim's and Marshall's outstretched hands, completing the circle once again.

There were moments during the next five to ten minutes when one or two of us were so close to contact that we could taste it, but for reasons best known to powers greater than our own the whole thing ended without a successful contact being made. The circle broke up and the night's efforts were at an end.

"I just don't understand it," Jim complained to himself. "I was so looking forward to speaking to someone tonight. I was so sure." His thoughts, expressed aloud, continued as he wandered out of the room and away.

To no one's surprise Marshall said nothing, he just acknowledged us one by one with a glance, maybe a slight nod, and then he too went on his way.

Jaqueline seemed quite unmoved by the lack of success so too departed without a word, in fact without so much as a glance in my direction. I don't know whether anyone else got better treatment.

Disappointment tends to quiet people down.

Strangely, it is at time of such disappointments that people could best benefit from conversation. It is one of those things. That's human nature for you!

Daryn seemed a little upset by the whole experience. Being as young as he is I think he misses the familial connection more keenly than the rest of us. Renee smiled at me as I stepped over to Daryn, she left me to try to say a few words... Not something in which I am well practiced.

"It is very disappointing."

He had remained seated, but looked up, maybe a little surprised at being spoken to.

His eyes were filling up.

"You know this does happen. Sometimes it can be several visits between contact," I explained.

"But my family were never believers in this," he said softly.

"They don't have to believe, Daryn. If we can break through the barriers then we make them believers."

"I just hate knowing what's going on. I think it'd be easier if I didn't," he explained. "And knowing the most important person to me needs me more than ever."

"It isn't easy, but we do get through to them sometimes," with no reaction from him it seemed I wasn't making my point. "And when we do, then everything becomes so much clearer."

"My friends and I used to do stuff like this... We used to try to contact the dead. It was fun then. Nothing ever happened though."

"That was fun, this is serious. It does work and it works both ways," he was calming down. "I promise you, we will do it. Who knows you might even get to walk through your family's house... Jim did that once." His eyes lit up.

"Really. He passed over completely?"

"You bet he did. I was right here and watched him move between here and there, he spoke directly to his son."

"I wish I could do that. I wish I could tell everyone that I am alright. There's someone who really needs to hear that."

"We all have people who we need to speak to."

"He blames himself for what happened. Fact is," the eyes started to well up again, "I'd have done anything for him. He needs to know I don't blame him."

I put my arm on his shoulder. "No one ever said being dead was easy, but we manage. As you will."

After a few minutes we left the old cottage together and talked for a while, an experience that wasn't completely weird but it was strange... I mean there's not much call for conversation here...

MICHAEL EWERS

WHAT YOU WISH FOR

I wonder how many of you truly believe in Guardian Angels.

It can be difficult for you I know, but if it helps I can say to you that we do exist, we always have and always will. But we always seem so under-used: I guess that is why when someone asks for our help we try our best to get stuck in and make it happen.

Here's an example for you, Jerry. Jerry was a lovely man: I say was because he soon became very bitter. Not at all grateful. Let me explain.

First of all, you need to understand that Jerry was a fat man. I don't mean that unkindly, simply as a statement of fact and expressed here in HIS words.

It was a simple fact of life that had dogged him from childhood: initially it was a few too many sweets from mum, then it became the easily brushed aside teenage puppy-fat before becoming simply a weight problem when he hit his late teens and then on into adult hood.

With the constant reminder of how unhappy he was with his lot in life Jerry was in his own words a triple chinned, double-bellied now nearing middle-age man who had more to look back on in life than to look forward to and who was not enjoying the efforts he made, time and time again to control his weight.

One could in all fairness say that genetics had given Jerry a kick in the teeth right from day one. So many people refer to being over-weight as being the result of over-eating, over-drinking, not exercising, eating the wrong things and so on. Some even say their genetics are at fault because mum, or dad were also fat. In Jerry's case, it really was true that genetics was the foundation of his misery – genetics had made him weak: weak willed. A total distaste for most things healthy, a bordering on nauseating obsession with full sugar Cola and anything Cadbury's meant he would be consuming calories at a rate normally reserved for four-legged beasts of burden, ironic as he was the creator of his own exceptional weighty burden.

Time and time again the target would be set: nothing drastic, not something unmanageable or unachievable... Several times a year he would set his target of losing 10kg in the space of 2 months, maybe 10 weeks... The soup diet was a disaster: there were no chocolate flavored soups, which left him limited to tomato soup – the one he could just about pallet, but which was always accompanied by excesses of French Stick bread with salted Welsh butter to taste.

The cabbage diet never started, simply because it contained cabbage.

Fasting was the ideal diet as he seldom had time for food when in work and had never really been much of a breakfast eater, it did however lead to considerable snacking, often Wispa bars, bought in a pack of four of course, on the way home in the car. All four consumed in less than 20 miles. In Jerry's world he made a huge improvement by switching to Wispa bars as they have holes in them, holes containing simply air, so they must be healthier and have fewer calories: everyone knows there are no calories in air, right?

The structure of such groups as Slimming World and Rosemary Conley had been explored but discreet observations of the classes from afar had always put him off: asking for help from a stick-thin beauty just was not going to happen. At least if she had some meat on her should have been able to relate to his situation! That was his thought process. Some might call it convenient excuses, but either way it was enough to secure a drive away from such places without having entered.

It was a matter of weeks before his 39th birthday when Jerry had a moment of clarity one night in bed: partly because he couldn't sleep, partly because he'd experienced about half an hour of indigestion that felt more like a heart-attack and partly because for the first time, his stomach was obscuring the ticker-tape along the bottom of the TV screen on Sky News... His stomach was actually in the way of the TV! Was he at that point? Choosing between food/belly and television!?

This was the evening that the thought of joining a gym first entered his head. As a thought it had tried to enter his head before, but his own self-defense, self-preservation systems had blocked the idea on approach to his ears. Now, in a moment of weakness it had got through to his brain and was actually being processed as a real possibility.

To someone new to a gym environment such a place can be daunting indeed: seeing the fitness staff from afar would probably be the decider.. He had already agreed with his subconscious that if the people in the gym all looked like Slimming World staff he wouldn't even cross the door. But to his surprise, looking in to the gym, there was a short woman of pleasant if somewhat slightly round proportions sat watching the people exercising and those people were a real mixed bag: no one was ever going to be as ungainly, over weight and unsuitable for exercise as Jerry: this Jerry had decided and would not be shaken from but there were some large people, one or two ugly people, one very old one...even one large, ugly and old person. Being able to put others down as a mechanism to elevate himself filled him with momentary bravery and he stepped closer to the door – this was a terrible mistake he realised almost as soon as he'd done it as his movement had triggered a reaction from the Fitness Instructor whose periphery vision must have been like that of a cat.

Within seconds the Fitness Instructor had coaxed him over the threshold of the gym door, had a reassuring hand on his shoulder, was smiling but was noticeably not talking prices. Jerry knew he was on a fast boat to gym membership but seemed powerless to resist. Seeing the reaction from the members of the public who were training as he walked in empowered him more: not one of them even looked up. Then he saw it: not exactly his dream machine but nonetheless a machine that could have been designed with him in mind. It was an exercise bike, but it had a huge seat, full back rest and built in Sky TV! He could sit, peddle and watch Sky News without his belly getting in the way. Just for an instant he was weak and as if some cosmic force was controlling everything this was when the Fitness Instructor pounced with news of a fantastic promotion running through 'til the end of next week.

It took a few days passing until his gym induction for Jerry to get completely the opposite opinion of the gym idea, to decide that comfort eating would console him and that after he had recovered from the shock of a recent gym visit, even if it was just to look around, that maybe swimming was more his type of thing.

It was swimming that brought him and me together for the first time: that is to say for the first time in a corporeal sense. I'd known him for all of his life, in some way you wouldn't possibly understand I knew him before then. Anyway, it was looking down over a swimming pool, the horrid humidity and smelling the chlorine that spurred me on to make a one-to-one contact and finally get to grips with the sadness this guy was carrying with him.

To say that Jerry was not the most talkative person in the world was an understatement, to say he was a bit of a loner, somewhat self-centered, an understatement but I knew the buttons to press and knew all too well that fighting the flab was the way into conversation. That poor self-esteem was the way to garner some kind of a rapport and to express pitiful self-worth would gain me a friend for life. If Jerry could find someone he could look down on from his lowly position then he'd grab hold with both hands and foster the friendship of a lifetime.

"I have always wished I could swim", I said softly, standing to his side.

No response.

"I am terrified of water... Get palpitations in a puddle I can."

Again, perhaps predictably, no response.

"I know two swimming teachers: still wouldn't get me near the pool though."

This time his head moved, ever so slightly. My ethereal-self was just as aware of how his eyes had moved, his heart beat changed slightly and how he'd taken a long deep breath.

"I am just not built for public displays of semi-nudity. So even if I could bring myself to go into the shallow end. Well, there's just no way."

"You see all shapes and sizes. And everyone is equal when they're in the water," Jerry stated, with such knowing almost self-assuredness I thought for a moment he might actually get of his backside sometime soon and go into the pool himself. Then of course, reality bit.

"Wouldn't be so bad if there wasn't this huge viewing area: everyone watching, children laughing, people pointing."

"We're watching," Jerry said, quietly. He turned and gave me a look: he reminded me in that moment of a mother looking at a naughty child, caught with his hand in the biscuit barrel…even I think of food when I am around Jerry.

"I think I would give anything to be able to swim."

"I would give anything to…" his voice was low and trailed off to nothing.

"I'd take 10 years off my life to be able to walk in there with confidence, jump in and just swim. Nothing fancy or record-breaking, just swim a few lengths."

"10 years?" he questioned.

"No hesitation"

"I have often thought I would do anything, absolutely anything to lose some weight. Just a few stone, nothing major…just enough to get me motivated."

That was his overriding wish in life. "A few stone?"

"I'd do anything…" he said with the solid determination of a chocolate addict.

"Well you never know what is around the corner."

We continued to watch the swimming for a little while and, unbeknown to him, I drifted away.

I decided that it was my job to help this weak-willed shadow of a man to achieve his goal.

It was the next day, while a morose Jerry was struggling to retrieve something from under his desk that smoke filling the office floor he worked on triggered the fire alarms.

Never one to rush anything and self-assured that this was a pointless drill, from under his desk, Jerry did not appreciate the urgency. When his office was checked by the designated fire officer, it was perceived as being empty. When Jerry finally retrieved his pen and struggled to rise his weighty frame from the floor, he got a whiff of the smoke that had by now almost cleared the building of staff.

Was it me or was it fate – if indeed we are indivisible – that arranged for him to trip on the leg of his chair and twist his knee? The crack it made as he went was less significant that the sharp snap of his head smashing in to the corner of his desk followed by a thud of this body falling to the floor.

His lights were out. No one was home.

When he did come around the flames were lapping around him and his trousers were just catching fire.

Stuck between his desk and a cabinet, trapped by a knee that screamed agony when he tried to move, a head that swooned and skin starting to bubble from fire Jerry screamed like a man possessed.

I am pleased to say that this Guardian Angel earned his wings that day.

I watched as Jerry's leg burned... I looked down on him as the Fire Service staff arrived and as they along with the Paramedics saved his life.

But they could not save his leg.

It took many weeks for him to recover but now, he is starting to get about a bit. And he does so with a far worse attitude towards his life than ever before.

I fear I may never understand humans.

You try your best for them and still they will not be happy.

One thing he wanted was to lose a few

stone in weight: that's about a leg, yeah? So I arranged for him to lose a leg. And he's still not happy.

BLISS

Carla was what some people, who wanted to be nice, would call a little ungainly.

It was by action rather than effort that she had obtained this unenviable reputation many years ago and, try as she did, she was unable to escape it. As far as outward appearance went she was the picture of normality, her hair was in a modern style, though nothing to attract attention, makeup was always worn to add effect to what was already there rather than to give her the appearance of a terrible warrior in war paint. Clothes were always well selected, accessories in perfect keeping with herself, her clothes and where she was. All should have been so much better, yet things were far from how she would have liked, how she wished, how she dreamed.

At the age of sixteen, Carla was employed in a local coffee house, just a five-minute walk from her home. The people there knew her, but not her less than perfect record. After having spilt the coffee once too often, tripped over a customer's pram and once having delivered a piece of steaming hot pizza into a man's crotch there had been no option to the owners other than to let her go. She had clung on to the job for four days.

By her seventeenth birthday she'd had five jobs, each one tending to be a little further away from home, not a purposeful attempt to move away from those jobs she'd already lost, more of a helping hand from fate.

At the age of eighteen she did what her parents had been dreading for years and started a course of driving lessons. Sheer amazement swept them both up as they watched their daughter return after each of her weekly driving lesson without having crashed the instructor's car and with herself in one piece.

It was a silly hope they had, that perhaps the 'Curse Of Carla', as they called it, might have been lifted.

For the first time in her life, Carla excelled at something practical and passed her driving test first time. It was the worst twist of fate that landed her in a hospital bed two weeks after passing her test after having been hit by a car while crossing the road outside her parent's home.

The driver of the car had been a businessman who'd enjoyed a little too much 'hospitality' at a works function before then setting about driving himself home.

After a few days in hospital Carla was very much her usual self, but hiding under a cloak of multi-coloured bruises, bandages and a plaster cast extending from her hand to her shoulder. But, having to remain in Hospital for observation was becoming a strain but that was all about to change.

It was this day, the first day that she had been able to get out of her bed to walk down the hall to the loo without being supervised, that the man of her dreams walked somewhat aimlessly in to her room.

As the door opened, the dark haired man's presence entered. It seemed a long slow motion second or so later that he himself entered. His head was bowed at first, maybe concentration, maybe something else, but when he looked up, Carla was physically jolted, her heart seemingly taking a leap. "Oh excuse me," he said, his smile broad and transfixing. "I was looking for my friend's room; obviously I've got the wrong one. I'm sorry to have disturbed you."

"That's alright," Carla replied. She amazed herself at being able to speak at all in front of a man who'd just walked out of last night's dream and into her hospital-room reality. "You didn't disturb me."

"These rooms do all look a bit the same sometimes," he told her, once again, he ended the sentence with that smile.

Again Carla amazed herself, she spoke and made sense, "Not from in here they don't." She smiled back to him.

That was the first time the two met.

They saw each other the next day when Carla walked once again to the ladies loos a few rooms away from her side room.

He smiled as he approached and she screamed inwardly at the joy of seeing him and then panicked at the thought of having to find something to say to him... She just had to get him to talk to her, for a moment she felt like a fourteen year old school girl with a crush, totally tongue tied and feeling herself break into a cold sweat.

"I see you are getting better every day," he said as he stopped, stood in front of her. "I assume you will be out of here soon?"

"The nurses can be quite persuasive," Carla told him, her mouth thankfully working while her mind was whirling.

"Do you mind if I walk back to your room with you?" he asked.

Carla stood silent. It had finally happened. The inevitable. Her mouth had stopped co-operating with her brain and her lustful thoughts were starting to take over...

He didn't wait for an answer, he stepped to her side and turned. "Feel free to take my arm if you need to..." he suggested.

Oh she needed to, but there was a nurse walking towards her and she'd probably get shouted at if she were seen being helped when she didn't need it.

"Is your friend recovering well?" Carla asked as they walked.

"They're letting him out later this afternoon, maybe early evening."

"So soon?" she asked, the shock in her voice possibly betraying her disappointment at the thought of no more accidental hallway liaisons.

"Well, you never know, perhaps he'll grow another appendix and have to have that taken out..." the guy joked. Carla looked away trying to hide her disappointment.

"You never know..." she said, regretting it immediately as a very stupid thing to say.

"Now which one of these is yours again?" he asked.

"Next but one... The door's ajar," she told him.

They walked the few final steps. Neither speaking. Carla worrying that these were their last few moments together.

"Well," he said as he opened the door to her room wider, "someone's popular."

On the movable tray-stand lying across her bed there was a basket-arrangement of flowers, white and lilac flowers topped off with a lilac bow. "my my... Boyfriend?"

"Hardly," Carla blurted out bluntly. Again, hating her mouth as soon as she had spoken. "Perhaps they've been put in the wrong room?"

"Don't you have anyone to send you flowers?" he asked, perhaps sounding a bit nervous.

"Well, no, not really. Dad does now and again," she replied pathetically. She looked over the arrangement, "They are beautiful, but they don't seem to have a card with them."

"Hang on a minute," he said and he stepped outside the room.

Carla separated a bit of the clear plastic that was protecting the flowers and took a sniff of their scent. She'd never had flowers sent to her before, well not like these. They were as lovely to smell as to look at, she savoured the moment in silence.

She was jarred back to reality, "The nurse put them here. They were delivered a little while ago, for you. The nurse had to sign for them so they know they're for you."

"But no card?" she frowned.

"Must have fell off... What does it matter? They are lovely. You like them. Enjoy them. They're yours!"

Carla sat on the bed and looked at them, puzzled, pleased but puzzled...

"I really should be off. It was really nice seeing you again. And I'm Scott by the way... I suppose I should have said that first."

"And I'm Carla..."

"So, uh... Well, Carla, if you see me when you're out and about, be sure to give me a wave, hey?" He smiled that smile again.

Carla smiled back, "You do the same," she said and then, with a slight wave as he passed through the door, he was gone..

*

To her surprise, Carla's parents denied all knowledge of the flowers.

Ready to return home a few days later, the flowers were resting on her lap like a prized possession as she was wheeled to the front of the hospital. She kept hold of them in the car on the way home and they were placed in her bedroom where she could see and occasionally smell them at her leisure. They were as bright and full of life as the first time she'd seen them and often the subject of speculation, her parents as interested to know the sender as she was.

Imagine her wonder when she got a telephone call from the hospital a few days after she got home, to let her know that another flower arrangement had been delivered for her and could she please arrange for it to be collected.

Her father made the trip for her and collected the flowers, which this time did come with a note attached. It read:

Dear Carla,

I hope you like these as much as you liked the last ones. Please forgive me for not telling you they were from me, but I was worried you'd think it odd - a complete stranger giving you flowers. They lit up your face... I wish I were there to see your face now. As I can't send them direct to you, I've sent them via the hospital..

If you can forgive my deception and would like to meet – dinner perhaps? Please call me if you'd like that...

Yours,

Scott x

Carla saw no telephone number. She flipped the small piece of paper over and there it was. She let out a sigh. Next to the number he'd scribbled the words 'any-time'. She smiled to herself and then explained the whole thing to her parents who were watching her as if she were crazed.

*

Carla wasn't the sort of person to make a man hang on - she'd never had anyone to hang on - but she did make a point of waiting until the next day before picking up the telephone.

She first picked up the telephone handset at about half past nine, just after breakfast. She had held it on her lap for a while without dialling. Eventually, she returned it to the small table where it usually sat and waited and thought and waited.

She re-read the note and wasn't sure what she should say. This was new territory for her, she'd never had a guy send her flowers before. A few biological throwbacks that laughably referred to themselves as boys had given her a few flowers in the past, but young teenagers do that. They'd thrust flowers held in a grubby paw at any girl who they thought might give them a chance to reach uncharted territory, but her territory was intact and she liked it that way. She was saving herself for someone who made her feel 'WOW!' and she'd met the first man to do that while she was in hospital... (She discounted Brad Pitt and Tom Cruise as unreachable).

She treated herself to a pampering bath and then spent a while doing her hair just how she wanted it and then spent an age on her finger nails, trimming, buffing, polishing... When she was happier in herself she felt more confident and so once again went to the telephone.

She dialled the number and waited.

It seemed to take a while to connect. There was a beep and a man's voice answered, "New Art, Scott here."

"Hello. Is that Scott? This is Carla..." she said nerves making her voice crack up.

"Carla," his voice was raised he sounded as excited as she was.

"Yes, I got the flowers and they are beautiful, really beautiful."

"I'm glad you like them. I am very sorry for not owning up the first time. I think I was embarrassed," he told her.

She imagined the look of embarrassment on his face and thought of how cute he must look. "There's no need. I know now," she told him.

"How are you then, I did call at the hospital a few days ago to see you but you'd gone home. It took me a little too long to pluck up the courage I suppose."

"If it helps, I'm very nervous too. I haven't done anything like this before."

"I suppose if we're both nervous that makes it a little bit easier..."

"I think dinner would be great," she blurted out, her mouth doing the more unusual less than well-mannered impersonation of herself.

"Good," he said back. "I can't really talk now because I'm at work. Can I give you a ring later, early this evening? Or do you perhaps fancy that dinner tonight?"

Carla could almost hear the fear of her negative answer in his voice, but she wasn't about to say no. All that talk from her so-called friends of years ago about how they should never be too eager and keep him hanging on, all of that went out of the window. "I think tonight would be perfect," she replied. She had regained her calm, dignified persona. She gave him her parents address and her telephone number in case of any change in plans.

*

The afternoon was a panic-stricken visit to the high street with her mother because, naturally, she had nothing to wear.

First choices had to be re-thought because she was walking with a walking stick and some dresses and suits just didn't seem to work with a cane in her hand. Should you colour-co-ordinate with a cane?

Even her mother was grateful when the outfit was chosen and they were on their way back home.

Another bath was had. The outfit was checked for the slightest piece of fluff and then put on. Hair was done, make-up applied. The clock ticked away and she stood, she moved to the mirror and then paced to and from the window. She asked the time a few times then added a visit to the grandfather clock in the hall to her little route. Now it was mirror, window, clock... Repeat...

There was a sound of a car, the dull thump of a door being closed and then she saw him. He looked so smart, the perfect figure of a man, striding towards the front door of the house. Her heart thumped, her eyes widened and her mind raced.

*

By night, the quaint little coffee house she once worked in, and was fired from, became an expensive, slightly exclusive, restaurant and it was to here that Scott brought her.

The evening was the picture of perfection in every detail for Carla, straight out of one of the romance novels she would spend hours reading.

When they entered a bow tie wearing man who seemed to know Scott already met them. "Good evening sir," he then nodded to Carla, "Good evening ma'am. May I show you to your table?"

Their table was well positioned along one side of the restaurant, they would not be crowded and would have the chance to see people as they arrived. Carla enjoyed a bit of people watching and smiled to herself at the view she would have in the event of the date not going too well.

They ordered drinks and browsed through the menu while making light conversation, which spanned Carla's schooling, Scott's attempt at college, Carla's love of trashy novels and Scott's addiction to pulp fiction stories. They each enjoyed walks and both seemed to enjoy making the most of their beautiful surroundings, taking drives through the mountains and the occasional picnic surrounded only by spectacular views. "Of course, I don't do that very often. You get looked at a bit odd if you're on your own..." Scott said, his look deep in to her eyes making the suggestion that perhaps she could accompany him some time.

By the time they finished their meal, slow-drank their coffees and talked, talked and talked some more it was getting dark. They'd enjoyed each other's company, oblivious to anything and everything around them for almost three hours.

Scott had stuck to mineral water throughout the meal and so drove Carla back to her parents' home where both mother and father had made sure they'd be in bed before her return home. All the lights were off.

"Can I convince you to come in for coffee?" Carla asked. "Or would that make me sound like a cheap TV drama?"

"You don't have to ask me twice," Scott said, switching the car off and undoing his seat belt in one swift fluid motion.

By the time Carla was out of her seat belt and about to grab the door handle, Scott was at her door, opening it for her.

*

In her mother's kitchen, Carla was so deep in thought she was almost unaware of Scott being in the room with her. Their conversation had halted as the noise of the kettle boiling got louder. She stood over the cups ready to do the pouring and let her mind wonder to the things she had only ever dreamed about, but which were now closer than ever before. She had enjoyed an evening out with a man who seemed almost too good to be true. He was stood about two meters from her and she was hoping that she wasn't just imagining his eyes bearing in to the back of her. What were her chances of a kiss? Should she excuse herself for a quick trip to the bathroom to check her breath? If he tried to kiss her, should she offer a cheek or her lips? Her nerves came back... She was jarred back to reality by the click of the kettle of water reaching boiling point.

"Forgive me..." Scott was stood right behind her.

She turned, they were toe to toe.

"...but if I don't do this now then I'm going to be a nervous wreck and completely unable to hold a hot mug..."

"Pardon?"

"I've been wanting to kiss you all evening. I'd rather not wait until I leave, if that's alright with you...?" he waited.

Carla was lost in his eyes for a moment, she didn't say yes. She slowly closed her eyes, leaned forward a little and let him do the rest.

She had already been aware of her heart thumping but now it was as if it was trying to affect an escape. She felt a sudden shortness of breath as their lips met... He took her breath away.

She pressed her brain to remember every fraction of this. The feel of his lips, softer than she'd expected. Their warmth...

When their lips parted, she realised that she was standing in darkness, her eyes still closed. She opened them slowly to see him too opening his. She'd read in one of her many magazines that you can trust a man if he trusts you enough to close his eyes when he kisses you.

By the standards of those magazines he'd already passed so many tests Carla could write her own article... One about meeting the perfect man.

When they did move from the kitchen, their conversation went back to something they'd just touched on in conversation at dinner, Carla's accident.

Each time the subject came up, Carla was sure she could see anger in Scott. He said it made him so angry to hear about people who drink and then drive. He told her so many times how lucky she was to be alive, able to walk. But then smiled about the silver lining to the cloud. Her accident had meant that they met.

Although she herself had convinced herself a little that she might have been in part to blame for the accident she listened as Scott outlined how easy it would be for her to take legal action, sue for damages. Not only the driver, but also the company he worked for who knowingly supplied alcohol at a lunch when they knew all their rep's would be driving afterwards.

Scott convinced her that she had rights. He

certainly left her that evening with a lot to think about. Firstly a civil action, secondly another date and thirdly another kiss which he gave her as they were standing at the front door willing the evening not to end.

*

Their second date went as well as the first and included a special piece of information from Scott. Having spent much time thinking about Carla's accident he'd looked in to what her best course of action might be and offered to help her with an unofficial approach to the company that employed the rep' that hit her.

He explained that a friend of a friend had had cause to use a company about two years ago that meets on your behalf to explore a settlement agreement in an attempt to bypass the need for any civil action. Though they have no power over any criminal charges or responsibilities they had a very high success rate and saved a lot of people the public humiliation of expensive court hearings.

He suggested that she consider it, purely as an option. He explained that the first consultation was free and the company operated a no-win no-fee arrangement. If they did secure a settlement she would pay a five per cent figure over to the company and all paper work would be done for her. She would simply have to sign on the dotted line a few times.

By the end of the date, Carla had given the matter enough thought and asked Scott to set up the first meeting for a time that would be convenient for him, as she wanted him at her side throughout.

That evening out concluded with a far more passionate kiss at the door.

*

The meeting was held and over in less than thirty minutes. Arthur, the representative of the company known as 'Civil Intervention' agreed to represent her as soon as she'd made the points of her case clear. When the word 'police' was mentioned, the man's eyes had seemed to light up. He was almost ecstatic when he heard that Carla had been hospitalised for just over a week.

The paper work would be prepared within forty-eight hours and a meeting sought with the company involved for as soon as possible, a meeting that Carla was not required to attend. She agreed to have 'Civil Intervention' represent her and leave everything in their 'capable' hands.

Their hour-long drive home seemed unbearably long. As the two of them held hands as Scott drove, they both felt their passions rising; Scott invited Carla back to his place for coffee.

Scott lived in a modern flat, which he called an 'apartment', complete with views, wooden flooring and decor that looked the work of a professional. A painting on the largest wall was an impressionist thing that Carla didn't understand at all, yet her eyes were drawn to it time and time again. His sofa was so soft she was sure she was still sinking further several minutes after sitting and the tiny details around the room were all just right.

When Scott went to the kitchen for coffee, Carla soon followed. She walked up behind him and placed her hands on his shoulders, "Forgive me," she said softly.

He turned, "Pardon."

"If 'I' don't do this, 'I'll' never forgive 'myself'," she kissed him full and hard on the lips and prayed that he would be kissing her back.

As the kiss continued, their hands started exploring each other until clothes were being loosened.

*

When they finally peeled off each other, in something of a heap on Scott's bed, they were both glistening with the sweat and breathless with the intensity of their lovemaking.

Scott rolled slightly, leaning on his elbow to look at Carla. "I've never known anyone like you," he whispered. "Would I scare you if I said, I think I'm hooked?"

She entwined her legs around his, smiled with satisfaction of her most wanted words heard. "I was hooked when you said: 'Oh, excuse me'!"

He ran his hand lightly down the full length of her torso, "Stay tonight. Please."

She pressed herself in to him, rolled him on to his back then climbed on to him. She kissed him, he kissed her and they began sweating all over again.

*

The following morning was something of a rush for both Carla and Scott.

Carla had to return to her parents' house for a change of clothes and an embarrassing talk with her parents, while Scott made apologies to his boss for having to take an unscheduled day off for personal business. They had been disturbed during breakfast by a telephone call from Carla's father asking them to contact Arthur at 'Civil

Intervention' urgently. When Carla called she was told that there had been an unexpected development that required her to attend their office at eleven a.m. to discuss a 'tactic'.

When they arrived, Arthur looked flushed with excitement and had them ushered in to his office immediately. He asked them to sit, asked them if they wanted a drink, they didn't, and then apologized for calling them in.

He explained, during the standard examination of the case facts it has been discovered that the company whose rep had caused the accident was called 'M 'n G', "The most important fact we uncovered was that they have been heavily involved in a government-run road-safety campaign backed by all major road-safety campaign groups and are heavily involved in a national advertising campaign that centres on three things: Car maintenance and safety, the misuse of mobile 'phones while driving and most importantly, the dangers of driving while under the influence of alcohol."

Scott and Carla exchanged glances.

"Our best estimates are that 'M 'n G Inc' is more than six months and four million pounds in to this project. If you give your consent we will use this information as a tactic to secure a quick, substantial, settlement. Which would almost certainly have a secrecy clause attached. I need to know your thoughts before I go in to this meeting this morning."

Once again, Scott and Carla exchanged glances, neither sure quite what to say.

"What is your advice?" Carla asked.

"My job is to get you recompense for the wrong done. In so far as that is concerned I have to advise you to use every possible means at your/our disposal to that end. You must keep in mind that these people acted in full knowledge of what they were doing, that they are responsible not just for injuring you, but for putting you in to a situation that could - but for pure chance - have killed you, or left you wheelchair bound for the rest of your life. Or brain damaged."

"You want to use this tactic then?" Scott asked.

"It's not solely about recompense now," Arthur explained.

"No? What then?" Carla asked.

"These people are publicly campaigning for one thing while openly doing another. These sorts of people only understand the power of the pound. If you want to stop them doing wrong..."

"But the campaign for road-safety... If they are exposed, then their campaign could fold and in the long run people could get hurt..." Carla said.

"We can give them the option of making good. Our silence will enable them to keep their contribution to the campaign. I'm sure they'll see that we're offering them a decent way out. We are only looking for fairness."

*

Two weeks later, Carla and Scott sat in Arthur's office for over an hour while he represented them in another office somewhere else in the building.

Arthur's P.A. came in to check on them regularly but never with any news as to how things were going.

As they became more and more impatient and Scott started pacing, Arthur returned.

Both Scott and Carla looked at him expectantly.

"They are consulting with their bosses. They wanted more time, a few days; I told them they have an hour. Needless to say they are shitting bricks."

"And after the hour?" Scott asked.

"I have had papers drawn up, in one hour they and I sign them or else I file my case against them, making public the details and naming the people individually: their firm and the individuals on the board. It seems two of them have in the past worked in an advisory capacity for the Ministry of Transport, the Safety Initiatives Panel. You should have seen the different shades of white and red in quick succession they went through..." Arthur laughed at his coup.

"I'm not finding this very funny," Carla said bluntly.

"Forgive me," Arthur composed himself as Scott put his arm around Carla. "Perhaps it would be easier, as I've told you before, to keep in mind we aren't pursuing individuals, we are opposing a company. Cement, bricks and floor after floor of glass. 'M 'n G Inc' is very large and we are today's minor inconvenience. Trust me, they'll have far more worries to deal with after we're gone. We'll be forgotten before the ink's dry on the documents."

The 'phone rang.

Arthur answered it, listened and then smiled smugly, "Is the liability form signed?" he paused as he listened. "Inform them that I expect to meet their legal team tomorrow without any excuses." He hung up.

He turned to Scott and Carla who were assuming the call was relating to them, "The preliminary form has been signed, it admits liability which is admissible as evidence. They have as good as signed the actual forms. Their legal team wants to meet me tomorrow to thrash out details, that's just as I'd expect. Everything looks signed and sealed. I think that's a personal record for me."

Carla leapt forward and hugged Arthur, then hugged Scott, he then hugged Arthur... It was quite emotional in a sterile sort of way.

"Don't either of you want to know how much your actual settlement figure is?" Arthur asked.

Carla looked at him, "How much?"

"Seventy five thousand pounds for negligence..."

Carla screamed when she heard the figure and jumped towards Scott whom she kissed...

Arthur continued "...Seventy five thousand recognition of culpability. One hundred thousand for personal injury and thirty thousand for the silence agreement. All in all, two hundred and eighty thousand pounds... Minus fourteen thousand for commission of course."

Carla screamed again, Scott was dumb struck and between the three of them there was much cheering, backslapping, hugging and a little kissing...

*

Neither Carla nor Scott actually met anyone from 'M 'n G Inc' face to face. Exactly seven days later, with the paper already signed, Arthur's secretary informed Carla that an electronic transfer of funds had been successfully completed in to the account she'd specified the previous day.

The whole thing was over and the relief was amazing.

Carla was so overjoyed she felt the need to get up, go out and spend on something. She had the urge to splurge.

Four hours and a matter of minutes after stepping in to a travel agent's on a whim, she and Scott were now boarding a plane for trip to the United States. Never in her wildest dreams could Carla have imagined the way in which her life was unfolding. Not so long ago she had been unaware of any particular future for herself. She'd had another dose of fate the like of which had dogged her all her life, when she'd been hospitalised. That low point was the point at which all changed.

At God-knows how many thousand feet up and while reclining in an unexpectedly spacious seat she sipped orange juice while holding the hand of a man the like of which dreams are made.

"I have something for you," he whispered as he leaned across to her. He'd been concealing a ring, turned around the wrong way on his little finger so as not to expose its' tiny pure stone. "Our one-month anniversary," he said as he slid it off his finger, showed it to her briefly before sliding it on to her second finger. "I was hoping we might find a beautiful sandy beach sometime this week, around about sunset if possible..."

Carla's eyes were wide enough to pop, her heart thumping with a readiness to escape. She was lost with surprise, shock and adoration.

"Will you marry me Carla?"

Causing a ripple of shock from other's sat around who hadn't heard the hushed exchange of words, Carla burst in to tears and they both fell in to each other's arms - as best as they could when sat in seats on a jumbo.

The warmth and tightness of his embrace was overwhelming.

"Miss! Miss, can you hear me?"

From that euphoria to horrible pain was such a short journey.

"She's coming around, she'll need another shot." So much noise: people were shouting, emergency service sirens blaring away.

Carla started to struggle: the tight embrace that had felt so assuring when it was Scott's arms around her was now an agony of an emergency services stretcher into which she was fastened, immobilised.

"Miss, you've been in an accident: a car has given you a bit of a bump. We need you to stay calm. Please try to stay as still as you can." It was the reassuring voice of a dark-green clad paramedic, who had no idea of the pain being endured. The physical pain was completely removed by medication, but the agony of a life time that had flashed through her brain in those minutes of chemical induced euphoria now dissolving into the reality of her real life was unbearable.

"She's getting hysterical, she'll hurt herself, we've got to sedate her", were words she heard faintly... She drifted off again.

CHILD WITH SPIRIT

Saturday 10th...

The short journey out of town to the Sugar Loaf Hospital was a pleasant one most days. For Richard Owen it was more pleasant than for most. The short drive took him through some of the classically Welsh country side, something he loved and appreciated so much more now, having spent so many years away from his home land.

Today's drive was a little tense.

Today was the day that his six-year-old daughter, Rachel, had been waiting for, for weeks. Today was the day of Bradley's party: he was now seven. In the last few weeks Richard had been asked more times than he ever wanted to remember, "how many more days dad?" referring to the approaching party. He'd sat Rachel down with a large-print calendar and tried to explain how each day was represented by a number. Each day a new number. He showed her where today's date was and where the date for the party was. Together they counted out that there were eighteen days to go. Rachel was satisfied for a few days. Then he'd had to sit her down again and this time added the use of a pen. He told her that she could keep the pen by the calendar on the kitchen worktop and every evening, just before bed she could cross off the number for the day and count how many days were left. He started to worry that she was a little too attached to this Bradley boy.

Once again, a happy routine was established and every night, like clockwork, Rachel would move a stool across the kitchen, put it at the counter, climb up and cross the number for today. Soon they were in the low-teens then down to twelve, she was more excited when the number got below ten and more excited still everyday there from.

On the Monday evening before the party, Richard took her to the local shopping centre as promised and together they looked for something suitable for this boy that Rachel thought so much of. Richard asked what Rachel thought they should spend, she didn't know. He suggested £10 to which she agreed and off she toddled. He watched from a distance as she went from one end to the other of several children's sections in several stores. Finally Rachel decided on an 'Action Man' toy which, as she pointed out to her father, is normally more than £10 but is less now: this particular item was on sale.

With the present bought, Rachel wanted to wrap it at once and when they got home that's what she did. She placed the precious item under her bed and was, thankfully, finally, content.

Today, Saturday, had started so well. Rachel had gone swimming in the morning with her aunt, which gave Richard a few hours to himself - much needed after a week coping as a single parent. Saturday afternoon came: Rachel rushed in without a goodbye kiss for her aunt and ran straight upstairs to get changed. Her party dress had been laid out days ago on the bed in the spare bedroom and even her father was forbidden from touching it. Indeed, after the dress, shoes, ponytail ribbon and all important birthday gift were laid out, he entered the room at his peril. And she'd always know if he had been in there.

She'd changed and presented herself to him down stairs with amazing speed and to be fair, this little six year old was quite able to present herself without her father's help. He was amazed and perhaps a little unnerved by how well she could cope at some things, even at this young age, without any help from him. It often gave him pause for thought.

She could tell the time and insisted that they should be early, wanting to see Bradley and give him his present before any of the other children did. It was lovely to see her so excited.

In the car, Richard explained once again what would be happening later, "Now remember, aunt Jenny will pick you up and bring you to the Radio Station. Okay?"

"I know Dad. You said," she complained.

"And what do you do if you want me or your aunt Jenny?"

Rachel sighed, frustrated at her nagging father, "I tell an adult that I want to speak to my dad and give them your 'phone number."

"And what..." he started to ask, but Rachel

rattled off her father's mobile 'phone number before he could get the sentence out.

"Good girl."

Most of the rest of the journey passed off with hardly any comment, the radio was on and Rachel liked just about every song, one after another, even singing along to one of them much to her father's amusement.

He parked the car and they both got out. He got the present from the back seat, which Rachel insisted on carrying and they started to walk towards the hall where the party was to be held.

"It's very quiet," Richard commented.

"We're early," Rachel informed him.

"Quick check. What do you say if some asks you if you want something?"

"Dad," she moaned.

"Let's hear it please."

"I say 'yes please', or 'no thank you' if I don't want it," she replied. A six year old, so tired of her father's fussing.

As they got to the building, they found it locked. "Too early it seems," he said to his daughter whose frown showed her anger.

"Excuse me," a man from a car parked nearby shouted over to them. "Are you here for the birthday party?"

"Yes. That's right."

"I'm sorry, the party's cancelled. The boy's mother has tried to contact as many people as she could and I'm here to catch anyone she missed. It seems the lad had a bike for his birthday and came a cropper the first time he rode it, poor thing. Think it's a broken arm."

Rachel said nothing.

She said nothing to the man when he said goodbye, she walked back to the car in silence and said nothing as they each belted up and her father started the engine.

"I'm sorry love. I'm sure he'll be all right; they'll probably have the party on another day. Perhaps in week or two."

Rachel said nothing.

"Is there anything else you'd like to do? I can cancel my show for today, if you'd like to go somewhere else... McDonalds?"

"I'll come to the Radio Station and see what new cd's they've had in," she said half-heartedly.

"We don't have to if you don't want to," Richard told her, but she wasn't interested in anything.

At the Hospital, Richard signed himself and his daughter in and then they walked back out, across the car park to one of the old residential buildings. The top floor was the temporary home of the local Hospital Radio Station where Richard put in a few hours voluntary work every week.

*

The Radio Station was dead, as usual on a Saturday. This was the one day of the week when nobody seemed to want to do a programme. There were people begging for a few hours on the week-days, several who did shows that went up to ten or eleven o'clock at night, one that actually started his show at seven in the morning, but Saturday was notoriously unpopular. It could be that people wanted to go shopping on Saturdays, that was a bit of a tradition. Maybe Saturday was seen as the day to be with the family, to take the boys to the football field and so on. Whatever the reason, Richard was seldom accompanied by anyone on a Saturday and he liked it that way. For all intents and purposes he had free reign. The Programme Controller would have recordings of his show but he'd seldom have to worry about having to talk to the stupid squirt who's accent made him the hardest person at the station to understand - ideal for Hospital Radio? He'd only ever met the Station Manger once and that was by accident because the woman had forgotten her glasses the evening before and as for the other presenters... He gave them a wide birth preferring to restrict his contact to the once or twice a year fund-raising events that everyone was supposed to attend and the annual awards night, which was mandatory.

Today was as usual, right up until about ten minutes before he was due to go on air. Reception put a 'phone call trough to the studio. "Hospital Radio, Richard speaking. How can I help you?"

"Hello Richard, this is Debra. I'm afraid I must ask an awfully big favour of you. I'm supposed to be showing a reporter around today. Someone from the local rag, Andy something, but I'm stuck in traffic. I'm still on the outskirts of Cardiff, there's no way I can be with you for the best part of an hour. Would you please see that this Andy guy gets in and just keep him here? We need the publicity if we're going to raise any more funds for our move."

"No problem, but you do realise I'm going on air in a few minutes. He'll just have to sit and do nothing, I can't watch over him."

"No problem Richard."

"Ok."

Thank you so much. And I will be there with you as soon as I can. Any problems, just give me a call on my mobile, the number should be on the chart in the library."

"Will, do. See you in an hour or so."

Rachel was in the studio as the call ended, "We're going to have a bit of company. A reporter."

"Are you going to be on telly?"

"No. This is a reporter for the newspaper. Because we are moving to the new hospital unit we need to get people to help us, hopefully by donating money. This reporter is going to come and listen to the programme and will meet the Manager and then if everything goes right, he might write a piece to put in the newspaper."

The 'phone rang again, reception letting him know that there was guest wanting access to the Radio Station.

Checking his watch, seven minutes and counting, Richard asked that the reporter be pointed in the right direction and he'd meet him. He left Rachel to go through a box of cd's.

As he walked through the car park he was surprised by a woman, obviously a reporter, walking towards him. She was quite a stereotype in some ways, carrying the pen and pad, large bag over her shoulder, dictaphone to her mouth that she was chatting into, quite at ease with the image she was creating.

The two met, "Are you Richard?" she asked.

"Andy?"

"Let me guess, you were expecting a forty-five

year old twenty-stone scruff who hadn't shaved for a week, who wears a trench-coat and chews on an old cigar?"

"No. I was told Andy, as in Mr," he paused. "At least I think I was told you were a 'he'."

"Andy with an 'i', A-N-D-I."

"No offence intended I assure you. Would you come this way? I'm a bit rushed for time."

"Really?"

"I'm due on the air any minute," he explained.

As they made their way to the building and up the three flights of stairs, Richard explained the change of plan and the missing Radio Station Manager. He apologized at every opportunity, hoping to keep the apparently easily offended woman sweet.

"If it means I get to see you in action it's no skin off my nose. In fact it'll give me an idea of the kind of stuff you people do up here."

"That's simple," they entered the main door in to the corridor off of which all of the Radio Station room lead off. "We broadcast music and chat that we think will be of interest to people in hospital. Patients, staff and visitors."

"Local funeral service rates. That sort of thing?"

"God no..."

"I was joking."

Richard laughed, a little nervous. "Those sorts of things do happen. By mistake that is. I remember the first programme I did solo, was of classic television and film themes. I thought oh, 'M*A*S*H', that was a good theme I'll put that on."

Andi didn't seem to get it.

"In addition to the General Hospital we

broadcast to, we go out to this one, a Psychiatric Hospital... The 'M*A*S*H' theme is actually called 'Suicide Is Painless'... That name is reflected in the lyrics."

Andi got the point.

They walked in to the studio; Rachel was waiting in one of the guest seats. "Andi, this is my daughter Rachel. Rachel, this is Andi. Andi's a reporter."

Rachel got off her seat and came over to shake Andi's hand, much to Andi's partially concealed amusement.

"Are you going to sit in Rachel?" Richard asked.

"No thanks, I've heard your show. I wanted to borrow some paper please..."

"You help yourself and I'll be in to check on you after the first few tracks." Rachel left and Richard made himself comfortable behind the console. "Make yourself comfortable. As soon as I've got everything sorted over here I'll be free to talk."

Andi sat in one of the guest seats and watched as Richard pressed switches, turned tiny knobs, checked sound levels, cued three cd's and fiddled with a strange box that seemed to use 1960's cartridges. Suddenly the sound of a BBC news broadcast came through the studio speaker.

"That's our sustaining service, for when we're not actually on the air ourselves. When the news finishes, I jump in just before the next BBC programme starts. If I get it right, the listener shouldn't realise that they've switched from a multi-million pound state-of-the-art studio in

London, to a rinky-dink operation a hundred and fifty miles away."

Andi looked on, impressed.

"...and the next news is at three o'clock..."

One slider moved up, one moved down and Richard pressed a large green button. The laughable jingle announcing the station ident' rang out, Andi smirked when she heard it, as corny as it was.

Richard held a finger to his lips as his microphone went live and the programme began.

"Good afternoon, this is Richard Owen live from Sugar Loaf Hospital Radio. For the next three hours I will be with you, bringing you a look at some of the local news stories of the week, the sports results as they come in this afternoon and in amongst all of that there will be a great selection of music. And the music is all chosen by you, our listeners." He looked up from his complex desk, "We might even have a special guest interview a little later, if things work out right," Andi's eyes met his. There was fear in those eyes. "We begin with a track chosen by a young man in ward 3/3, specially for Andrew," music started, softly first but betting gradually louder. "This is Richard Marx, 'Right Here Waiting'," Richard brought the music up and his microphone down.

"Not bad for a 'rinky-dink operation'," Andi commented.

"Practice. So would you fancy making your Hospital Radio debut today?"

"Ask me again later," she replied with a smile, and an inward shudder.

The show continued. Andi was quite flattered

that some of the local news included were actually some stories she'd written. Richard flattered her style and managed to get a nervous yes to his suggestion that she allow him to interview her later.

"You're quite welcome to get yourself a tea or coffee. I can't offer to get you one sorry," he gestured to the mixer desk, "Kind of needed here."

Andi got to her feet, "Yes, I can see that. Can I get you one?"

"Not right now thanks, drinks strictly prohibited in here. But you carry on, down the corridor first door, just by the entrance."

Andi used the time it took for the kettle to boil to have little look around. There were five doors, and therefore she assumed five rooms all of which lead off from this one short corridor. The first room, by the entrance was a tea-room, or at least had the basics for making tea and coffee. Next to it was a makeshift studio, lots of complex looking equipment that was noticeably older looking than the stuff in 'the' studio. At the far end was a locked door; a small sign said 'OFFICE' so she assumed that was the Manager's Office. Down the other side was the studio Richard was now in and the library which went around the building in an 'L' shape. As she walked in she was surprised at its size at first but then even more surprised by the thousands and thousands of singles and LP's that lines the walls. "Wow," she said out loud.

Rachel looked up, "Hi."

"Hello Rachel," Andi walked over to where she was sat. "So what are you doing to keep yourself amused?"

"We're drawing," she said. "I like to draw the covers of the new cd's so if I ask Dad to buy one he knows what it looks like."

"That's nice. So do you record them here and take them home to listen to?"

"If daddy's not in a hurry then he records them for me in the studio after the programme," she replied, still concentrating on drawing a small blue alien that dominated the cover of the cd in front of her.

There was a moment during which Andi wasn't sure what to ask. There were quite a few things she wanted to know, more so about Richard now than about the station. "How long has your dad been doing a programme here?"

"Since I was a baby."

"Quite a few years then." No response. "How old are you? No let me guess... You must be older than four, because your taller than my friends little girl... I don't think you are ten yet though. So somewhere in between?"

Rachel smiled slightly, "I'm six."

Andi's eyes started wondering over the room, "Do you ever help your dad with his programme?"

"He sometimes lets me pick a song for the end. But mostly the music is what the people in hospital want to hear."

"Does daddy go and visit the people in hospital then?"

"He goes on a Friday after he finishes work. He only works mornings on a Friday. He goes to see the sick people and then he picks me up from school," Rachel explained.

"What does your dad do? Where does he work?"

"Daddy works in town. He makes calendars and things."

Andi thought better not to push any further for the moment so allowed a few moments to pass and then changed the subject a little. "Wouldn't you prefer to be out playing on a Saturday afternoon?" she asked, quite unaware of the glare her question brought out on Rachel's face.

"I was supposed to be at a party," she said bitterly, her frown was back and her cheeks were suddenly quite flushed. A stack of cd singles that had been on the edge of the table fell to the floor.

Andi had been looking at and then past Rachel just as they fell, so didn't see quite how they came to fall. There was a crack of a pencil being smacking hard on to the table as Rachel got off her seat and started to pick up the cd's, most of which were open, one or two of the discs out of there cases completely.

"Oh, never mind," Andi said, fearing that Rachel might be upset at the mishap. "Let me help you with that."

"It's alright, we can manage. They have to be in order for the box." Andi noticed the case that the cd's seemed to be kept in. There was list of titles on the side, each one numbered so she assumed they tended to be kept in some sort of order. She bowed to Rachel's knowledge. "I was making myself a drink of coffee. Would you like something?"

"No thank you. I usually have a cold drink from the machine in the canteen when daddy has his break," Rachel replied. She continued to match discs to cases and set discs apart from each other.

"Are you sure you wouldn't like me to help. You might get your dress dirty."

"It's my party dress. It doesn't matter now," Rachel replied.

"You do look very pretty. Your dress is beautiful and it matches your hair band too..."

"I know." Rachel looked her straight in the eye. "I picked it."

Andi turned away so that Rachel wouldn't see her smiling, unsure whether she was about to laugh out loud. A six year old with better dress sense than her in her late twenties!

She left Rachel to her clean-up operation and went to see if the kettle had boiled. It was boiling away with some force, building up enough steam to switch itself off as she entered the 'tea-room'. There was a tin labelled tea, one labelled sugar and a small bed-side-cabinet-size refrigerator where she found some milk. With the sugar, tea bag and milk in her cup she started to pour the boiling water but almost scalded herself when the kettle suddenly lurched, almost losing her grip. An adrenalin rush flowed through her, she got the kettle back down on the table in one quick movement and stepped back realising how she'd just come close to a nasty burn.

She rubbed her hands and then gripped the kettle once again, paying more attention to what she was doing and took her time.

With her tea made she returned to the studio and edged the door open slowly so as not to disturb Richard if he was about to speak on air. He noticed her and gestured not to come in with the cup, she placed it on a small shelf in the corridor that various keys were hanging off and then gestured for permission to enter.

"Everything okay?" she whispered.

"Fine," he whispered back.

"Good."

"Why are you whispering?" he asked with a laugh.

"Isn't that what I'm supposed to do when I'm in here?"

"Not unless you really want to," he replied in his normal voice. "You found everything you needed then...for the tea?"

"Oh yes. You know us women, give us a kitchen and we'll find our way around it..."

"I didn't say that."

"You wouldn't dare. Can I ask you a question? Something personal?"

"Sure. But I might not answer you."

"I was just in there," she pointed, "the library. Chatting with your daughter Rachel. She's a very lovely little girl."

"Yes she is. And your question would be...?"

"Does she often refer to herself in the plural. 'We' instead of 'I'?"

Richard seemed almost crestfallen, "Give me a sec'," he brought his finger to his lips and then brought his microphone up. "Time for some back to back tracks now. We begin with one for Laura who works in the maternity ward. Hello to you all down there. Now this song is one Laura heard some time ago, she couldn't be sure who sang it but knew it was called 'As If We Never Said Goodbye'. Now Laura, the only version I've been able to find is performed by the one and only movie star Glen Close." A huge fanfare erupted from the speakers as the track began, then the music died down, "I hope this version will be alright Laura. And coming up after this 'All Time High' for Carol who is hoping to be in labour right now and then a little something for a young man who asked not to be named... You know who you are..." The music came back up and the singing started.

"How do you time it like that? Just enough to say to take you up to when the singing starts."

"It helps if you know the songs, but the trick is to talk quickly, clearly and in short sentences."

"Must take some practice. How long have you been at this?"

Richard paused, "Six years."

There was a silent moment.

"I was asking about Rachel."

"When she's upset or angry, she does tend to retreat a bit in to a bit of a fantasy... She has an imaginary friend who pops up from time to time. When she's upset or angry usually. That's when 'I' tends to turn into 'we'."

"Arh. Well that seems simple enough..."

"Personally I hate it. I've tried to get through to her on the subject but when she's in that frame of mind there's no getting through to her about it."

"My brother used to have an imaginary friend. It's quite common."

"In my opinion these flights of fancy are a way for kids to try to get away with more than they usually can. Something goes missing, 'Gideon must have taken it'. Some thing gets spilled, 'It's not my fault, Gideon pushed it over'."

"She's named him Gideon?"

Richard loaded another cd in to a deck and started to pull his earphones on, "Yep."

A few minutes passed, Richard made a few more links and read out some local news from the regional news pages off a computer screen.

"I suppose you will be quite glad to get away from here?" she asked.

"Well, I'm half and half on that. I know some people feel as if it's the end of an era and all that. I think that what's important is that we get the programmes out there, to as many people as possible. This place won't be here for much longer so move we must."

"Have you seen the new unit at the hospital? Where you're moving to?"

"Only from the outside."

"I'm sure it'll be quite an improvement. Being so close to the General Hospital as well, that must make things easier. You visit the wards Rachel tells me."

"I try to, most weeks. You see, and this is strictly between you and me, there's an element that thinks working here is a license to just turn up, play a few of your favourite tunes and then go home with a big self-satisfied pat on the back. If we are really what we claim to be, a service for the patients and staff, then they should have a say in what we play. It seems like common sense to me." He started to fill in a few boxes on his play sheet.

"I agree. It makes sense."

"We are in the minority, though."

"So how did you get involved? It doesn't seem like the sort of thing you just happen across."

"My wife and I had quite a few requests played when she was in hospital having Rachel. After," he paused. "After that, I came here to see the station, had a chance to thank everyone here 'on air' for their kindness and was invited to come back anytime. And I did."

Richard's whole demeanour was different. He was suddenly less carefree and aimless in his body language.

"Have I said something wrong?"

"No. Not at all. Just remembering back to then. It's not something I do too often these days."

*

Andi allowed the conversation to go pretty much wherever Richard wanted it to go from there on. Her journalistic instincts gave her no particular sense of a story waiting to be told, so she sat back to wait upon the arrival of the Station Manager, Debra Waite. She tentatively agreed to a brief interview on-air shortly after three o'clock and allowed her mind to wonder on to the sorts of subjects she might raise. Should she simply ask questions or should she ask a few? Would she be able to ask any if she's the one being interviewed? She'd never been on that end of an interview before... Should she have a paper bag with her to stop her from hyperventilating with nerves or was she being silly? It was only Hospital Radio after all. Who the hell's going to be listening?

She thanked herself silently for not voicing that out loud.

"...It is now exactly twelve minutes to three o'clock so as is usual at this time we have a few comedy excerpts. These bits of fun will take us up to the hour and the news at three but I'll be back with more music of your choice and a chat with local reporter Andi Cassel. Any budding reporters out there wanting to know how to get into journalism...stay tuned..." His microphone came off and the voices of comedians of years ago began. Andi thought she recognized Kenneth Williams among them.

"This is when Rachel and I usually go across to the canteen. There are a couple of machines over there that sell snacks, fruit, drinks and stuff. Would you like to join us?"

Andi looked around the studio, "You're just going to leave this?"

"Sure. We'll only be a few minutes, this tape runs for ten. We'll be back in plenty of time," Richard explained.

"Perhaps I should wait here in case the manager arrives..."

"Actually, strictly speaking I'm not supposed to leave you here on your own. But, well," he smiled, "I'm sure I can trust you... Just this once."

"Why, thank you for that vote of confidence. Anyway, you trust me enough not to swear live on air don't you?"

Richard didn't answer; he smiled and went through to the library to find Rachel.

"Can I get you anything?" he asked a few moments later when he came back, holding Rachel's hand. "Bar of chocolate, apple, yoghurt?"

"Thank you, no. I'm fine."

"We'll only be a few minutes."

The sound of the transmission was all that could be heard. There was a speaker in every room, though only some were on. There was one in the locked office; she had heard that when she'd walked past. There was one that seemed to be broken or disconnected in the tearoom, the studio speaker were turned down quite low, but she could hear the one in the library. There was a sudden burst of laughter, which she hadn't expected, having not been paying much attention to what was being transmitted.

She walked through to the library.

The pictures that Rachel had been drawing caught her eye. There were several very distinct styles of drawing. Some were obviously the work of a six year old, some seemed markedly better and some as good as one might expect from an adult.

She was suddenly struck by the dissimilarities and then by the numbers. She'd drawn, she counted them, fourteen and was in the middle of number fifteen. That's only a few minutes per drawing. And some were so neat. With most six year olds they don't know how to colour within the lines properly, some were as expected, but others were very neat.

Andi suddenly felt cold. It was a noticeable movement of cold air as if someone had opened up every window at the one end of the large room and a wind was blowing freezing air towards her.

The fully open large heavy wooden door to the library started to creek and then to bump up against the wall. She spun around as it thundered closed, causing the entire room, it felt as if it maybe the entire building, to shake. To her own fright she screamed.

She ran to the door and opened it.

As the rational side of her mind knew, there was no one there.

She turned, the door moved to close again, this time the force caught her on the side of the head and knocked her to the floor.

She didn't move.

*

"Blackcurrant? Are you sure?" Richard asked.

"Yes please," Rachel replied.

"Go on then."

Rachel pressed the button, there was some buzzing and whirring, then a can of drink thudded out of the machine.

"I think I'll have orange," he put some more money in and got his drink. "How about something to eat? You didn't have any dinner because you were going to the party. And you didn't have much breakfast because you were going swimming. You should eat something."

Rachel scrunched her nose up as she looked over the offerings in the machine. There were small trays of chips, which could be heated in the microwave that was supplied. She was never one for fruit at the best of times and the only chocolate on offer had coconut which she hated.

"I tell you what, as soon as the show's finished we'll go and get some food, okay?"

She was happy once again. "Chicken nuggets?"

"Whatever you fancy. Come on," he put his hand on her shoulder and they walked out of the canteen, down a short corridor and out of the building. There was a small courtyard to cross and then they rounded the Radio Station building.

"What do you think of Andi?" Richard asked.

"She's alright."

"She enjoyed talking with you earlier. I think she likes you," Richard said. "Thinks you seem very bright for your age."

"Do you like her?"

"I think so. But..."

They climbed the flights of stairs and entered the long corridor that was central to the station. Andi was sat on the floor rubbing her head.

"What happened? Did you fall?" Richard asked rushing to her and helping her to her feet.

Andi noticed the scared look on Rachel's face. "I'm fine, really. The wind made the door slam and it caught me by surprise."

"Wind? It's a spring day, all sun no wind..." Richard started to argue.

"Well I didn't just walk in to it."

Richard moved her in to the library and got her to sit down, "Rachel, get me a paper towel from the tea room, wet it a little for me."

Rachel ran off.

"You're going to have quite a bruise there, I can see it already," he told her. "Are you sure you're alright? How many fingers am I holding up?"

Andi waved him to put his hand down, "Don't be daft. I'm fine. I've had a lot worse in the line of duty, trust me."

"Really? Been watching any drug barons recently then?"

"No, but I did catch a guy out who was claiming benefit and was working as a gardener. He claimed he couldn't walk more than fifteen steps without a sit down. He made all this fuss about the D.S.S. calling him a liar, got our paper to do a big piece on him. Then we get an anonymous photograph of him carrying sacks of pebbles, the stuff people put on their drives. Well, that was it. My editor hit the roof. He wanted the full works. Pictures, stake-out... The guy spotted me one morning, threw a damn great garden gnome at me, I had to have five stitches."

"Sound like a dangerous job."

"He was one of the softer ones."

"Well, perhaps you should stick to something less physically demanding."

"I don't have a caring man to look after me so when my editor says jump I do. Or I can stop to ask 'How high?' but only on a good day."

Rachel returned with two paper towels, one wet one dry.

Richard applied the wet towel to Andi's head for a few moments, "Best keep this applied for a while. Just give me a few minutes then I can get you to casualty."

"No. I'm fine, it's just a bump," Andi protested.

"You were on the floor, you could be concussed or something," Richard argued.

"Your show, you've got another hour to do..."

"I'll go to the news at three and that'll have to end the show."

"We're leaving early?" Rachel asked, sounding a little annoyed. "I thought we would be here all afternoon."

"Rachel, I think making sure Andi's okay is more important," Richard tried to explain.

The words didn't seem to go in, but before he could try another tactic he noticed the door to the library was knocking repeatedly against the wall.

Andi turned slowly, recognizing the sound from earlier.

Rachel started to laugh, "Gideon's crying," she pointed and laughed.

The door slammed shut with fierce force once again. Again the whole building seemed to shudder under the force of it.

Richard, who had been kneeling by Andi, got up. He walked towards the door, "I don't want to hear that name again today young lady," he said pointing at Rachel. She knew when her father meant business.

The door wouldn't open. He put some weight behind it but still, much to his surprise it wouldn't open.

He hit it with his shoulder and it opened a little but slammed shut immediately.

"This is kind of what happened to me," Andi said. She stood at his side, ready to add her weight to his next attempt.

Together they propelled themselves into the door, which offered no resistance at all. The door seemed almost to have been flung open independently of their effort. They went through the open space and landed heap-style in the corridor just as the station manager came through the main entrance.

In the midst of checking they weren't injured, both Richard and Andi found themselves looking at each other. Such close quarters were new territory for them both and rather than being uncomfortable it was in fact exhilarating for them both.

"When you are finished rolling around on the

floor," the Manager said acidly, "you can get on with your show. I believe that's dead air I can hear."

They picked themselves up and each checked that the other was uninjured. Only then did Richard bother with his programme. As he entered the studio, the Manager stepped up to Andi.

"You wouldn't be the reporter I'm expecting?" she asked.

"Andi Cassel. Yes," Andi replied, extending a hand that the Manager accepted as if it were covered with something quite unpleasant.

"Debra Waite, Station Manager. I apologise for not being here when you arrived. I assume that Mr Owen has shown you around. May I ask what you both found so fascinating about the floor?"

"Actually we were locked in the library... Well, I don't mean locked as such, rather we couldn't open the door. It just slammed."

Miss Waite didn't look appeased, "It just slammed. You were locked in."

"We had to force it open," Andi continued.

"Perhaps if we go in to the office we can discuss the story you're here to do," Miss Waite suggested. She had the key out of her pocket and in the lock before her sentence was spoken.

The news at three started and Richard stepped out of the studio, "I do think you should have that looked at," he said as he went past them in to the library. "Just to be sure it's not serious."

Miss Waite looked at the slowly darkening bruise on Andi's head, she raised her eyebrows.

"The door kind of slammed by itself earlier too. I was in the way of it at the time," Andi explained.

*

Rachel was sat, arms folded across her chest. She was pouting and shaking slightly.

"Rachel, I want you to come in the studio."

"Gideon won't talk to me. You were cross at him and me and now he's cross at me."

"Rachel, we've discussed Gideon before now haven't we?"

"Doctor Sarah said that if I want to talk to Gideon you shouldn't..."

"I am here right now, not Doctor Sarah. And right here and right now I am telling you there is no Gideon. If there were then I would be able to see him. I can't, therefore he's not here. You're just pretending that he's here."

"He slammed the door when you said you were going to make me leave early..." she replied.

"Rachel, that was the wind."

"You always say that. You say the wind closes doors, blows things over. I know it's Gideon, he thinks it will make me laugh," she turned to look over her father's shoulder. "But it won't. He isn't clever. It's just silly," she shouted.

"Rachel," he grabbed her by the shoulders. "Who do you think you are talking to?"

She shouted and pointed, "Him, Gideon. Silly, stupid, Gideon."

Richard looked around him there was no one there, but Miss Waite and Andi were now stood in the doorway. He realised that he and his daughter had probably been making a bit of noise.

"That's enough Rachel. Now come on I want you in the studio," he extended a hand to her. She looked at him. She didn't take his hand but instead walked past him towards the door.

Rachel's back arched a little and she was propelled forwards. Screaming, she slid to the floor.

Her father was at her side almost as she landed.

"This place is weird," Andi commented.

"I for one will be damned glad to get away from here," Miss Waite said. "The place has always given me the willies and it will be no great loss when the bulldozers come in and the whole place is razed to the ground..." Her face lit up, "Now there's an idea. I wonder if we could have the place blown up like they do with those old chimneys and tower blocks. I'm sure that would raise some money."

Rachel was now on her feet and being escorted in silence past both Andi and Miss Waite.

"Rachel, are you alright?" Andi asked.

"Yes thank you, Gideon is a bully," she replied. "And I'm not coming here to see him anymore," she added, turning back to the empty room as she spoke.

She left the library and went in to the studio, her father a few steps behind, exchanging worried glances with Andi and to his own surprise with Miss Waite also.

*

"So Miss Waite, what's the history of this place?" Andi asked.

"This used to be an accommodation building." She gestured to the library's expanse as she came fully in to the room, "This was most likely the day room, where the three or four people who used to live on this floor would have their furniture, television and so on. What we use as the tea-room was a small kitchen but I don't think cooking was greatly encouraged because of safety. The other rooms were a communal bathroom and bedrooms."

Andi took all of this in while giving the library more attention than she had before.

"As I said, the whole damned place gives me the heebie-jeebies. I refuse to be up here alone after dark," she announced, shaking her head, which turned into a full-body shudder. "I don't like being up here alone in the day time."

Andi turned, quicker than one would expect. "Why?" she asked in such a way as to make it sound like a demand.

"Do you really need me to answer that question? Can't you feel it yourself?" Miss Waite walked to the centre of the room, "Come and stand here. Come on, stand by me, here."

They stood side-by-side, pretty much central to the large room.

"Just relax and tell me what you feel," Miss Waite said.

There were a few moments during which Andi did just as she was asked, then she realised what she had been asked, and the stupidity of it. She breathed in about to speak...

"The room doesn't have a feel," Miss Waite said. "Whenever you stand in the middle of a room you get a feel of it, sounds daft, but you try it somewhere else and I tell you you'll know what I mean. But here, there's nothing. If a room is capable of having a soul, this one has lost it. The whole floor actually. I've been downstairs a few times, the porter's night quarters."

"And..." Andi urged.

"And you can feel the room. Everything is fine and normal and comfortable and just as it should be. But not up here."

Miss Waite shrugged and started to walk away from Andi.

"So what exactly are you saying?"

"Every single person that I know that knew any of the nurses that stayed here has told me that the nurses involved requested new accommodations within days of moving in. Several resigned rather than live here. You draw your own conclusions Miss Cassel," she left and went back to her office.

When Andi followed moments later, she asked, "But what was this place before it was used for accommodation?"

Miss Waite looked at her in silence as she sat down.

"The building's very old, surely accommodation for staff wasn't its first use?"

Miss Waite, shifted in her seat, "Years ago, a woman who was found to be pregnant outside of marriage - and some who were married too I'm sure - could be placed in an asylum. For no other reason than she was pregnant out of wedlock. Did you know that?"

"That disgusting..."

"And if the family wanted to protect against the embarrassment of having a bastard child within their midst the mother and child could live out their entire lives in such deplorable circumstances. Surrounded by the criminally insane, the psychotic... Needless to say, not many children survived the environment. The healthy people who came here in those circumstances soon developed emotional problems of their own. Few ever left." She paused. "This building was for women in the last stages of pregnancy. The library used to be the ward."

"Up three flights of stairs...?"

"Which they were required to walk up, perhaps in the hope of inducing miscarriage I'm told, but that sounds too barbaric, even for these old places."

"That's unbelievable," Andi said in a horrified whisper. "If it were fiction it would be bad enough but..."

"And still the place reeks of pain and confinement, of desperation, hatred and supreme loss. It has the air of hell about it."

They remained silent for a while.

"Gideon's a child," Andi said under her breath.

"Yes," Miss Waite agreed. "And Rachel is sensitive enough, being so profoundly close to the feelings of loss herself. She taps in to him and he into her."

"You should stop her from coming up here," Andi suggested.

"I can't do that, Richard is a valued contributor. Nothing like what I get the impression has happened today has ever happened before. And how would I make that request?"

"Rachel speaks to Gideon regularly."

"Much of which I'm sure is the typical invisible friend thing that children go through. But it's buoyed up by a real something that she can really see and hear when she comes up here."

There were footsteps and then Richard was at the doorway, "Rachel's upset so I'm going to go to switch to the sustaining service... Then we're heading off home. Unless you want me to do anything different that is."

"That's fine, we'll be on our own way pretty soon," Miss Waite said. "Is Rachel going to be alright?"

"I think it'd be best to get a bit of distance from here. I'll speak to you tomorrow, but I'm thinking of taking a break until the move to the new studio. It's nearer home, more convenient..."

"Probably a good idea," Miss Waite said, her words laden with a knowing edge.

They were disturbed by words being shouted by Rachel in the library.

Richard went to check on her only to find her in an apparent tug of war contest over her drawings, but the opposing force was completely invisible.

Rachel shouted, "They're mine, you have yours."

Rachel, let go all of a sudden, the papers flew backwards and whatever was pulling them seemed to move back with force enough to tip a chair and slightly move a table.

"Rachel, time to go," her father said.

"Serves you right," Rachel sneered in typical six-year-old style.

An unseen force propelled the bunch of papers up in to the air.

"Now Rachel," her father shouted.

Andi and Miss Waite were now in the doorway.

Rachel stomped towards her father, "I'm never coming back here."

The lights in the library flickered, and then exploded in a shower of sparks.

Although it was daylight outside, the room was significantly darker now, the small windows required lights to be on even in the summer months. As the room settled, everyone was paused, waiting to see what happened next.

Miss Waite squealed, as she was pushed by the door of the library being closed.

"This is ridiculous," Richard sneered as he strode to the door and but his weight against it.

From their places on boxed shelves, a whole section of LP's exploded in to the air, almost all of them smashed as they hit the floor, the force was so great.

A second crackle and bang and more LP's were flying out of their places... Hundreds of them were airborne and smashing to the floor amid a torrent of noise, which increased over a period of seconds until it became painful. Smoke started to fill the air, the windows rattled and other bits of furniture started to move.

Amid all of this, Rachel remained calmer than the adults, seemingly quite aware of the movements of the tormentor, watching as it/he moved around the room, pushing furniture, grabbing records and pulling them into the air.

Miss Waite grabbed Rachel, Richard and Andi forced the door.

When the door opened, Richard and Andi held it open for Miss Waite and Rachel to pass and then followed.

The noise and confusion of the library remained there. As nothing seemed to follow them in to the corridor they all stopped in spite of their natural instinct to run.

Eventually they were all turned to see the chaos. Smoke, debris, smashed records, un-spooled tape, the occasional glint of a cd and other things swirled in the room amid a sudden and eerie silence. It was as if an action sequence was playing out with a volume control turned down. Any doubt of the supernatural nature of what had been occurring ended abruptly with all sound as the mayhem continued.

"This Radio Station is finished. Here and today. We re-launch when the new studio's ready," Miss Waite said firmly. "Now, I don't know about you people but I'm out of here."

"How do we explain this?" Richard asked.

Thursday 15th...

Richard entered the offices of the "Regional News" and asked the receptionist if he could see Andi Cassel.

"Is this about an article?" he asked.

"Definitely," Richard replied.

"If you'd like to take a seat I'll see if Andi's in the building."

When she did show up, Richard got to his feet. "I'd like an explanation about this," he flung a copy of the paper at her. She missed it and it fell to the floor.

She picked it up and read the bottom of page story headline, "'*HOSPITAL RADIO CLOSED BY*

POLTERGEIST'". She looked up to from the paper, "You don't agree?"

"This story will destroy whatever failing credibility Hospital Radio has in this town. It will also direct undesirable attention towards us, both as a charity and to the members. Not to mention Rachel. What the hell were you thinking??"

"It's a damned good story. A true story and there's no mention whatsoever of your daughter, or you," Andi replied, defensive in both voice and stance.

"Story? What about the people whose lives you disrupt, just as long as you get a story? And as for Rachel, I am the only member of that station that has a young daughter. You say this happened on Saturday last: well I'm the only person with a show on a Saturday. Anyone could work out who was there and who you mean by 'young child'."

"We are getting only good responses..."

"I bet you are."

"There's been a 20% increase in hits to the web-site. As a charity you must appreciate that a high profile help any fund-raising potential."

"How much fund-raising buys back respect? What's the price on a child getting picked on in the playground and having to be sent home from school in tears? How do I explain to Rachel that her 'friend' was actually some kind of horrible ghost?" he paused...leaned closer. "I've spent years telling her that ghosts don't exist. Can you imagine what it is like at three o'clock in the morning when she wakes up crying?"

"I understand that you are upset and angry but you can't say that anything in there is inaccurate..."

"You understand?" he asked, stopping her mid-sentence. "You really think you understand? Shove your story and shove your paper. And you can shove your opinion too." He turned and left.

Andi swallowed hard and then turned to face a considerable audience that had gathered.

Saturday 22nd

"...and if I could just add, the future of the new home of Hospital Radio is looking good. Indeed the station as a whole is looking good, thanks in part to the unexpected contributions we have received from around the world. I have never been a fan of the technology and until a few weeks ago hadn't sent or received a single email. Since the strange events that surrounded the slightly premature closure of our previous studio however, I and the station have received over four hundred emails, letters and some telephone calls. As a result we have now collected over five thousand pounds from people and companies - as a result of which we have managed to get back on the air in just six weeks. I have already started and will continue to reply to every single message personally. Without exception we have had messages of support and thanks for the service we supply."

Richard shifted in the new comfortable, swivel, reclining, chair, knowing that the recording was about to end.

"I wish to thank everyone, you know who you are, unfortunately you are far too many to name individually, for the work you've put in. Setting up the new studio, clearing the old one, installing some very complex equipment, dealing with people like me who can't even change a fuse. We owe you a great deal, and we will repay you by continuing to provide a completely free service of music, entertainment and news to the patients, the staff and indeed the visitors to our Local Hospital. Here's to a second fifteen years of the Abergavenny Radio Service."

A small round of applause sounded the last few seconds of the recording, over which Richard spoke, "That was Hospital Radio Station Manager Debra Waite speaking on Friday afternoon at the official opening of the new look Abergavenny Radio Service." The applause died completely. "Coming up in the next hour of the programme a selection of music chosen by you plus a few words from several of our presenters. I've spoken to quite a few of them over the last few days and asked them what the future of this service means to them and I must admit to getting a few unexpected answers. We'll be getting to them shortly, first up though is a track for Rachel, it's called "No Matter What"..." the music started.

A red light flashed on the console in front of him, it meant there was someone at the door.

He looked over to a small black and white screen. The security camera just inside the main door was showing him Andi Cassel waiting under an umbrella.

He sighed. "Crap," he said under his breath.

Before he had got to his feet, Rachel opened the studio door, "Andi's here Dad, shall I let her in?" she asked.

He tried not to make it too obvious to his

daughter that he wasn't pleased to see Andi, "I suppose so," he said. "But make her wait in reception. Tell her I'll be with her as soon as I can."

*

When Rachel opened the security door, they exchanged a few pleasantries. Andi was sure that Rachel would have harboured no grudge about the newspaper story, she hoped that the same would be the case for Richard, but she doubted her luck.

"Dad says you should wait here," Rachel told Andi. "He's doing his programme and he's still mad at you so he might make you wait."

Andi was taken aback by Rachel's bluntness. "Well, I have tried to apologize to him Rachel, but he's always out or busy whenever I try to speak to him or see him."

Rachel raised her eyebrows as if to say 'What do you expect?'

"Are you cross with me Rachel?" Andi asked.

"My friends made fun of me in school," she replied. "My teacher told us we shouldn't talk about silly things."

"And your teacher is right," Andi told her. "What you read in the papers is written to make people buy the papers. That's all."

"Everything's better now. We've been away to see my nanny and granddad."

"Oh, good. Did you have a good time?"

"Yes, and daddy did. He fell over at the beach and got all wet," Rachel started laughing. "At first he was cross then too, but granddad was laughing so much we all started laughing."

"I wish you'd had a camera with you. I think I would have liked to have seen that."

"You can come through to the library with me if you like. Daddy won't mind as long as we don't disturb him."

Rachel led Andi through to the new library. A far cry from the old one. Half the size, newly carpeted, comfortable seats, a computer terminal and professional looking cabinets filled with hundreds of cd's, not a single vinyl disc in sight. "This is much better isn't it?" Andi said as she walked in.

"We like it," Rachel said as she sat at a table and once again took up her drawing.

Andi paused for a moment, then let the idea drop. No, normal child invisible friend stuff, nothing to worry about she told herself.

"Andi." Richard was at the door to library. "Would you like to come through?"

Andi looked to Rachel, made a face as to suggest she was a little scared, Rachel smiled, and then followed Richard through to the studio.

"What can I do for you?" he asked, sitting himself behind the console desk.

"Two things," Andi said, bluntly. She sat on one of the high stool opposite the presenter's position, on the other side of the control console.

"Firstly, start taking my calls. Any chance of that?"

"If you have something to say we're face to face," Richard said, equally bluntly.

"I want you to admit that as wrong as I was you were also wrong to come to my office and say what you did. If it weren't for my story this place wouldn't be open yet."

"Ends justify means?"

"I didn't say that."

"The station is grateful, as a part of the station that means I am grateful. On any degree of a personal level, as a father, I think your actions were unforgivable."

"I see."

He put his finger to his lips to ask her to be quiet as he introduced the next track. When it was safe to talk freely once again he continued. "Now, you said two things?"

"The other one's moot now."

"I see."

"I was thinking that if you forgave me for long enough you might be able to get to know me a little better over a drink or dinner. I'm not difficult to like. But as I say moot now..."

She slid off her stool. "I'm sure Rachel can show me out." She left the studio and went back to the library.

*

Rachel was talking happily about something, Andi couldn't hear what, "Rachel, would you mind showing me out?"

"Have you got to go already?"

"Yes. Your daddy and I have had our little chat."

"I thought you might stay a little longer," Rachel said, a little disappointed.

"Andi has to go now Rachel," Andi turned, Richard was behind her. "But I can show her out." Their eyes met.

As Rachel watched her father and Rachel walk off, her face became serious, "Well I do like her."

All of the papers on the table flew sideways to the floor.

"Gideon. Don't! You promised," Rachel said in an urgent whispered anger.

GIDEON (masc).   Hebrew... 'Destroyer'.

MICHAEL EWERS

THE TRUTH WILL OUT

My Dear James,

The fact that you are reading this means one of two things. That somehow you have managed to get your hands on this by mistake and if that is the case then I beg you with all of my heart that you stop reading right now and either destroy this document immediately or else put it somewhere safe until you can personally place it in to my hands. If this isn't the case then the only other way by which you could be reading this is if I have died and you have started the task of having to go through my various papers and other effects.

It must be quite unnerving to have this now, it is effectively me talking to you from beyond the grave. As hard as it might be for you, that is exactly what this is designed to be. You see I do hope that it is the latter reason by which you have come by this. Simply because what I have to tell you here is something that I could never bring myself to tell you while I was alive. We were always a good team, you and I. I must warn you though that after you have read this, and you need to, trust me, you may think terrible things of me James. All I can plead is that you somehow understand that this is the only way I could possibly tell you the truth about your mother. You know we never discussed her: that is my fault I know, it just hurt too much. Perhaps, I say with the twenty-twenty vision of hindsight, I should have considered how much hurt you were feeling, and continue to feel, knowing so little of her. How could I ever have expected a baby to carry any memories through into adulthood? It was unacceptable of me to think you could. I cringe at the realization that I had the power to change that. As I sit here now, I lack the strength. I am so sorry.

I have been plagued by the knowledge that if anything happens to me and I haven't given you this information, which you have a right to, then you will be diminished as a man and I will have failed even more so in being a father. This is the easy way out for me. In my defence this is an unusual thing for me, for I hope that one thing that I have taught you is to do what is necessary, what is right. I hope I have not instilled in you a sense of doing things the easy way. For the easy way is so seldom the right way.

I am not going to bore you with all the details of my time with your mother, I will explain to you a bit of the woman she was, the relationship we had and the things that broke down that relationship. I will try to be concise, not so much for you but for me, for that may well be the only way that I can get through this. I will then try, I swear it, I will try my utmost to put into words the events of the final night.

The first time I met Janine, the woman who was in time to become your mother, she was working for a book company. I was working at one of the many office jobs I'd had over the years, this one was for a local accountant. I was there straight out of school doing their basic administrative stuff. Anyway, your mother would come in usually at monthly intervals with her arms full of books that she would leave in the staff area for us to browse through. Anyone who wanted a book would make a note of what they wanted and leave their name, your mother would come back a week later, collect the order and the money and then distribute the books. I can still remember seeing her in her little van, horrible yellow thing that it was. She used to drive that van like as if she had a wasp in her hair and was fighting to get it free. I used to think it so funny back then, yet it is a miracle she didn't kill herself and a lot of others while she was perched behind that wheel.

After a few of her visits I got to know her a little. We would discuss little things of no great significance, not the weather, a bit more interesting than that. Give me some credit. One day she asked me if I'd look after the money aspect of the books for her. She wanted me to collect the money and make a note of people's orders and then she could ring up the morning before she was due to call in to check that she had copies of everything that people wanted. I was glad of a chance to chat to her. In truth I suppose I was dodging some of the filing if I was busy seeing to her, letting her in through the security door, making her coffee, chatting about the new books, counting the money for the orders, all these little things. You must understand that I was never a dater when I was at school. I knew a few girls sure, everyone did, but never went 'out' with them. Not properly like on dates, so this was something special for me.

I loved the days when she would call. Unfortunately the arrangement didn't last. A few months later she called in and during our conversation she said that she would soon be moving to a new job. We both thought that there would be one more visit before she left, but that wasn't to be. I can still feel the emptiness of seeing her drive off in the van, even though I thought I'd see her once more. I can still remember that afternoon, one of the secretaries was joking with me about her. She kept on and on until she finally instilled in me the urge, the strength if you like, to ask this woman out on a date. I'd never done that before.

Days came and went, I wasn't expecting to see her. Weeks came and went and my intention to ask her out grew. A month passed and she hadn't been in. Six weeks was about when I realised that she wouldn't be coming back and then one day, while I was stood looking out of a window waiting for the kettle to boil, I saw the yellow van. My God did my stomach flip over. I thought it was trying to turn my navel into an emergency exit or something. I started waving like a complete fool as the van parked and then the driver emerged; a young stick insect of a man, who I thank God even to this day, didn't see me waving at him. I avoided him and settled in to my life once again.

Almost two years after this fiasco, and a few

short-term jobs later, I started work for the local Housing Department. I had only been there for about two months when I met her. Completely out of the blue. I was walking down the corridor on the ground floor and wasn't too aware of what was around me until I was just a few steps away from the Personnel Officer that had interviewed me for my job. I acknowledged her and then saw Janine. I was gob smacked. Firstly she looked totally different with much shorter hair but also because she was wearing a business suit. I think they used to call it 'Power-Dressing'. We said hello in passing and I heard her saying something as she moved off into the distance, '...I know him...' or words to that effect anyway. Needless to say I wanted to know whether she got the job and got my answer about twenty minutes later when the Personnel Officer found me and told me that the young woman I'd seemed to know had got the job she'd applied for. She was to be working in the Grants Department, which was attached to the Housing Department which meant I'd get to see her regularly. If nothing else the two departments shared the same canteen.

Several of the guys liked her when they saw her and quite a few of them hit on her in the canteen, but I was the one whom she invited to sit next to her and I was the one who got up from her side a while later having secured a date with her. The other guys were all watching for the signs of me striking out and passed a few consolatory comments as I passed them. Unable to conceal my grin they were silenced without me saying a single word.

The next few months were spent getting to know her. Here are a few of the facts which may sound a bit daft now, on paper, but they were wonderful little pieces of information for me, each one extracted for the purpose of getting to know this piece of loveliness even better. Your mother was five foot eight, don't ask what that is in metres I really don't know and have never cared. Her hair was pale ginger, almost blonde in the summer and she never once in her life dyed it. Her parents were both dead when I met her but had been business partners for almost their entire lives owning a corner shop in their home town of Knighton - you may want to visit the place one day but I'm afraid I haven't a clue where in Knighton the shop was and shortly after her parents died it was converted into a house: your mother went to school in Shrewsbury, her father would take her every morning in his mobile shop and she would come home by bus or sometimes by car with a friend. Her favourite subject in school was English. Your mother loved to read, unfortunately she would often find the stories of love through adversity more compelling than the more taxing stories I like but our differences drew us together. She loved pastel colours, I like the primaries. She liked classical music and jazz - not that I've ever classed jazz as being music - while I preferred the popular stuff, whatever happens to be on radio one at the time.

After over six months of dates, your mother and I conspired to go away on holiday together. I say conspire because we didn't want people knowing. Now you're quite right, I'm sure you're asking what would it matter if people knew... Well, firstly your grandfather was still alive then and he was an old fashioned sort of man. The idea of the two of us off on holiday together...the important facts being that we were going together - alone together - and that we were a couple but not a married couple...would give him some serious problems, maybe even a seizure. Secondly there was the fact that a lot of people we worked with knew we were dating but we weren't making it obvious just how serious we were about each other. I suppose in some ways we weren't making that too clear even to ourselves.

By today's standards, our little break was nothing. But we had a long weekend on the north Wales coast, we were each other's world for those few days. All the time we were there we did things that we wanted to do and got to do them with each other and, well let's be honest, those few days were when I came face to face with manhood. If you know what I mean. And boy oh boy was I eager to arrange for another long weekend away... But I'm getting ahead of myself. Our break was better than either of us imagined and I think somewhere deep inside we both used it as a guide to whether we really had any kind of future together. If we could spend every minute of every day together and enjoy ourselves and each other as much as we did, then there must really be something special there. And there was.

Seven weeks later, your mother cornered me in work and bustled me in to a stock room. I thought this was going to be fun but my world started screaming at me from every direction within minutes. She was 'late', if you know what I mean. Well, we are talking a few years ago and plenty of women have children outside of marriage, but neither of us thought like that - not to mention my father's reaction, which I dreaded - I can honestly say with my hand on my heart that my first reaction was that we should marry and do so immediately.

Your mother was over the moon and at lunchtime we went to look at rings. We didn't need to tell anyone about it, we were spotted by someone at work. I had knowing winks and pats on the back as soon as I was back in the building. We both told people that we'd been engaged for over a month but didn't want to tell anyone until we'd found a ring. They all fell for it. We also decided that we wouldn't tell anyone about the pregnancy, but rather we'd change the dates a bit making everyone think the baby was due a good month or so after it was really due, add to that the idea of pretending to everyone that the birth was early and we had a chance of getting away with people not knowing that we 'had' to get married. It was a bit of a leap but we thought it best to try.

My father was overjoyed and I told him that Janine had always had her heart set on a Gretna Green wedding. Making it clear to him that we both wanted to be married as soon as possible, he eventually came up with the idea we were trying to get him to suggest: that we elope straight away and just do it. Surprise everyone.

I had already sorted the idea out in my mind, Janine had said she agreed so I made the suggestion as if asking for Dad's approval. We all have Friday off work, catch a train to Cardiff and then make our way north. It would take most of the day but it would be a fantastic experience. We could get the marriage arranged for Saturday, apparently they're very quick up there and there's no need to book weeks in advance if you don't want anything too fancy, then make our way home as a married couple on Sunday.

As I sit here writing and I'm sure it is the same for you as you are reading this, it sounds a bit fanciful, with a touch of the fairy tale about it, but that is how it happened and Dad came along too, he was to be my Best Man. The three of us arranged it and did it all in complete secrecy.

Now, time passed on and nothing came of the baby. After being fobbed off a few times I finally insisted on accompanying your mother to the Doctors and that was when the whole thing came out. There was no pregnancy, there had never been even a hint of a pregnancy. She'd fabricated the entire thing. Well, as you can imagine we rowed in spectacular style for quite some time. At the end of it, it all came down to her fear of losing me after we'd slept together on that short break. Maybe I was guilty, as she suggested, of making her feel used. I never did so with any intent, but she felt as though she had nothing left to give up to me and that I was more likely to move on. The pregnancy was her way of keeping me.

Over the next few months we rowed a lot. At the bottom of it was the simple fact that I just couldn't trust her. If a woman who claimed to love me as much as she said she did was able, was capable, of lying to me on something as big as that and then prepared to go through with a marriage all based on this lie... How could anyone trust someone in a situation like that?

She similarly got it in to her head that, as I didn't want to spend much time in her company, I must be seeing someone else. The mixture of all of this kept boiling over in to rows and then one day she grabbed a bottle of whatever was closest and downed the lot in front of me. Luckily, what she took would only have made her very ill, but all the same we spent couple of days in the hospital and she went on to a prolonged course of therapy. This was the first time that your mother tried to take her own life and yes I'm sure that I must shoulder some of the blame for it. In my own mind however, even now, I still place all of the blame squarely on her shoulders. Her lies, her deceit were the catalysts of her own troubles. Not me.

During the course of her therapy, which I was heavily involved with myself, we both grew closer. There were times when our lives started to feel like they used to. The therapy ended, she was a far happier person and started a new job that got her out of the house, meeting people and so she started to rebuild her life and I settled to the idea that perhaps my life wasn't so bad after all. At this point, you're possibly asking why we didn't just divorce and get the whole thing over with? Well, there were a few arguments before when the subject came up and during the therapy sessions we discussed it at length. The truth...? We were very much in love. It was her lie and entrapment that caused me my problems with the marriage. It was her own insecurities that caused her problems. Staying together even after all that had happened was evidence of our love, reason for both of us to realise what we had in each other. I don't know if that is enough to answer the question, but it is all I have.

Things were much better, but there were still low spots. I wasn't aware at first, but I soon came to realise that your mother had started drinking. She never got drunk as such, but she never had a meal without wine and never watched a film in the evening without a drink by her seat. I realised months later that she was downing alcohol every day and while I doubt that she was an alcoholic, she was definitely attached to the stuff in an unhealthy way.

Inevitably I approached the subject with her. My way was the most tactful I could come up with. I allowed the stock of alcohol in the house to go right down. I stopped buying the stuff that meant that she would have to buy it. I hoped it might dawn on her just how much she must be drinking if she was having to constantly buy the stuff, but no. She was buying wine and spirits almost daily. I arranged an appointment with the counsellor we'd seen previously and asked for some advice.

"Have you tried to talk to her about it?" was the first response. "If she's turning to drink then it symptomatic of other problems in her life." The result of the meeting was that I should try to talk to her about it but not be surprised if it was all my fault. And to think I had to pay for that thirty minutes.

When we did discuss the subject she became very upset, she felt her life was empty, that made me feel great, and that she wanted to do something more with her time. I told her I'd support her and that seemed to be that. She was overjoyed, I mean, too overjoyed. Strangely so. But the drinking diminished noticeably, she changed her job, enrolled in evening classes at the local college and once again everything seemed great with the world.

A few months after all of this was over, your mother asked me to come with her to the Doctors. She refused to tell me why which started my mind working on a whole series of horrible scenarios but what happened was fantastic. Life changing. Even to this day. While we were there, the Doctor confirmed what she already knew but what I'd never even thought about. Your mother was pregnant with you.

Your mother was a whole new woman throughout the pregnancy. She was glowing, full of energy and never once complained like so many women seem to about their swollen ankles, aching back and raging hormones. She was a truly perfect mother-to-be.

This changed when I discovered that once again, perhaps as a result of being a little more housebound, she was drinking. I couldn't believe that she could do that. Drink while pregnant. Yet again we talked this whole thing out. She needed outside interests and we found some that she could do while pregnant without causing any harm to herself or you.

Those last few months of her pregnancy, the birth and getting to know you my son are the few months that define my entire life. Your mother as I will always remember her and you, a miracle that I was to be reminded of every day of my life.

During the first few weeks of your life, my father, your grandfather passed away - thankfully peacefully - in his sleep. During this period your mother's health dipped quite a bit. The hormonal changes that a woman experiences, the depressions that some get after giving birth and the death of my father to whom she had become attached almost as if he were her second father, all conspired to knock her time and time again.

With your mother on strong medication and a baby to see to, I was forced to hire a Nanny to help. And this was perhaps the worst thing of all that I could have done. The Nanny, Catherine, was a woman a few years younger than me who seemed to fly around the house like an Angel. You, the baby, were always calmed by her, the house always looked after. Not that it was her job, but she provided the much needed something, to keep everything flowing. Janine thought she was a wonder at first, but then started to resent how the baby, you, would take a feed from her and not from his own mother. How the nanny was making the meals which she had always done - sexist by today's standards as that may sound - and an array of other things that all built up.

Things were taking an unexpected twist outside of your mother's awareness also. Catherine seemed to show some interest in me. At first I thought I was misreading her but her, I can't say 'advances', they never were really 'advances', but perhaps her 'attentions' became quite clear. I had never been in a situation whereby someone was showing me this overt attention before and certainly not in a situation in which I couldn't respond. As much as I might have wanted to.

As your mother started to regain her mobility, Catherine's hours were halved. Her attentions to me were so flattering that I found them difficult to repel and I think your mother picked up on them.

I began to realise that your mother never seemed to leave Catherine and myself alone. I was so split on how to take that. Was she watching me, or helping me to resist? Either way, after another few weeks we terminated Catherine's employment and that was that.

At least that should have been that.

I went to her house on my way to work the next day and apologized for the quick decision to end her contract. She was well paid and didn't seem to mind but I minded. As I told her, totally out of character for me, I would miss having her around.

She was taken aback, she was embarrassed about her previous advances and was sure that I'd made my disinterest clear. But I corrected her. She asked me in but I couldn't, I was on my way to work. I suggested lunch, somewhere where neither of us knew anyone. I couldn't believe it: she actually said yes. It felt amazing.

I got to work on a high. But started to doubt what I was doing. Was having dinner with someone you know, of the opposite sex, cheating? I was concealing it. Surely that made it cheating?

Lunch was amazing and as we parted she kissed me gently on the lips. My heart pounded, my mind raced and other parts of my body did their things too.

The afternoon flew by. When I got home, you James were having a running battle with your mother over your feed and she was drinking from a bucket-sized glass of red wine.

I asked the simplest un-confrontational thing I could think of, "What can I do to help?"

Your mother thrust you at me and screamed, "Get this little shit to feed," and disappeared in to the bedroom with her glass.

To my shame the things I did the next day changed the course of my life, and as much as you might hate me for it, I must say that the change was one for the better.

I was up early after a night of seeing to you every few hours, your mother wasn't seemingly any the worse for her drinking the night before, but if she was going to have a hard day then the least I was going to try to do was to see to you through the night...for as long as I could. It was sometime in the middle of the night that I reassessed my life, my life with your mother and my life with you. For some strange reason I was also thinking of a life with Catherine.

I went to the local shop to get a newspaper, it wasn't my usual routine but it would give me a chance to call Catherine without danger of being overheard by your mother. I arranged to spend the day with her then called work to say that I wasn't well and wouldn't be in that day.

Catherine and I had an amazing day. We started by having breakfast at 'The Bridge Inn', which has some of the most awesome views I've ever seen, and then we ended up booking in and spending almost all day in bed.

As I sit here, remembering the days I had with her I find myself quite stuck for words as to how that woman made me feel. The long weekend away with your mother a few years earlier had made me feel like a man for the first time. Well now I felt like so much more, it was like I was high on life and wanting more and more. More of her. When we had to leave I did so with the same feelings as that day when your mother had driven out of my life in that awful yellow van, but with the added bonus of knowing that this time, with this woman, we would meet up again and within the next few days. After so much crap over the last few years I finally felt as though something in my life was right and yet ironically, being a married man and newly a father, I also knew and know that it was wrong.

Understandably, I was dreading getting back home. I drove around a little to kill some time to make sure I got home when I would normally be expected. I was not surprised to open the door and be welcomed by the sound of crying from your nursery. I was surprised to find Janine unconscious on the living room floor. Of the bottle of whiskey stood on the table, less than a quarter of the contents remained. The Efexor she'd been taking for her depression were all gone, three empty strips on the floor suggested she'd taken up to forty-two of them. Another strip, one I didn't recognise lay beside them, Zopiclone, whatever that was.

Leaving you to cry on, I dived for the telephone and dialled 9 - 9 - then stopped... I put the 'phone down.

Everything in my life was on pause.

I looked at your mother and thought of the toxic cocktail swilling around in her stomach, I felt her neck. I couldn't be sure how long it was since she'd taken them, her pulse wasn't strong. I shook her a little, she didn't stir.

I looked at her, then the 'phone and waited. I had never had such a decision to make.

Then, without knowing what had happened in between, I was standing over your cot, I picked you up quietened you down and grabbed your bag of nappies, wipes etc and left the house for a while.

I drove around for a bit, dazed and then decided to go and see Catherine.

I explained that your mother had ignored me when I got home, I presumed she was drunk so just grabbed you and your bag of stuff and went for a drive. I told her that I thought she might like to see how you were getting on and she believed the lot. In part it was true, I like to think so anyway.

I had something to eat there, so did you and then I tried to convince Catherine that we, I and your mother that is, needed her services for just a few hours a week. Catherine was reluctant but agreed to come and discuss it with her. We both thought maybe a few hours out in the daytime could make a difference. It took some doing to get her to come back to the house, I had said that I thought your mother was drunk, but she agreed after a little friendly coercion.

Of course, her real job here was to be at my side when I returned home and found your mother who I was sure would by now be dead. Or not far from it.

When we got to the house she used her bit of First Aid training to assess your mother. We called for an ambulance and she took charge of you while I went with your mother to the hospital.

Your mother never regained consciousness.

With a history of mental health problems and having tried to commit suicide before there were questions about why she had been left in the house with such an amount of medication. I had made it clear that the house was clear of medication, especially the Paracetamol that had been your mothers chosen method of suicide previously. I hadn't been aware that she had a stock of Efexor, as far as I was aware she only had the strip she was currently using. As for the other, the Zopiclone, I didn't even know she had been prescribed that. I was surprised to find out that it was a sleeping tablet: she'd never had trouble sleeping.

That my son is a truthful account of the highest and the lowest points of my time with your mother and a clear illustration of why I have never been able - nor do I ever imagine myself ever being able to discuss it with you in person.

Beyond that time, Catherine moved in with me as Nanny and lover for a while but our situation didn't last long. She continued to act as a Nanny to you until you started school. I am sure that you remember her. It's years since you've mentioned her but I'm sure you do remember.

By the time you have read this I will have had to make my peace with a far greater power than I ever conceived of in life and will have had to answer for my actions. For my inaction. I hope that even if forgiveness is beyond you, that maybe a certain degree of understanding exists.

If there were ever one thing for me to leave you it is this: you've heard of the saying that the grass is greener on the other side of the fence. Never was a truer word spoken. Oddly, that grass seems greener no matter which side of the fence you are on. Remember that when you see something that is better than what you already have, and remember the down falls of wanting.

I never told you how proud you make me, you are the one thing that I did right in my life. I love you my son, and I will always watch over you.

Love,
Dad

LIFE'S REPRIEVE

PART ONE...

Marcus Stapleton knew the road like the back of his hand: he had travelled it twice a day for the last twelve or so years. Every so often, usually when he was considering whether it was time to start looking for a new job, he would try to work out roughly how many times he had actually driven it. Twelve years, that was twelve times three hundred and sixty five days, assuming three hundred days as a more manageable figure he would get to a rough estimate of about three thousand six hundred days, round that up to say four thousand five hundred and then multiply by two because he travelled it twice a day, once each way. Somewhere in the region of nine thousand times he'd travelled this damned road. Each time he did the mental arithmetic, usually six months or so between, the figure would have jumped and each time he would be spurred on to do something about it. If there was one thing he did hate it was the daily grind of the same old thing. Get up, put the cat out, have breakfast, shower and go to work. That was half of his life. The other half was: arrive home from work, shower again because he hated the thought of having any of the air his clients breathed out actually on him or his clothes and then settle down to a taste-free microwave dinner before an hour or so of television and then bed. Possibly having remembered the cat, but not always. This was his life.

In the last few years, in the last four years actually, since his last 'serious' relationship, he could count the number of dates he'd been out on, on his fingers. If he included a strange woman who claimed to be a clairvoyant the number was seven. The clairvoyant had got up half way through the starter of their meal and announced that she could just feel that they weren't meant to be together. She had a 'vibe' from somewhere 'not-of-this-place' that if they stayed together neither of them would be happy and just left. This was typical of the way his dates seemed to go and so for the last eighteen months he was observing a no-dating policy, getting his kicks from satellite television porn and anything with a chocolate coating. Of course what he dreamt about was the mixing of the satellite porn and the chocolate with a gorgeous brunette who would do his every bedtime bidding and who would also be edible in all the right places.

Other dates sprang to mind. He regretted opening up the entire train of thought now. There was the six foot two blonde whose makeup just had to have been applied by her two-year-old daughter... Or at least that was what he thought until they were in the car, outside her place, discussing the possibility of 'doing this again sometime'. Then he realised that she had actually put the makeup on herself. This was when he noticed the join in the hairline that the hair was a wig and that she was in fact only a practicing 'she'! Soon to be a full blown 'she' he stressed but let's face it, if you want to go out with a 'she' then that's what you want and expect. A look-alike, a part-time 'she' was a totally different thing and Marcus made his point very clearly, loudly and with some physical force too. If he could get his hands on him, her, it, whatever, now, then... Well, he had a few ideas about how to raise his voice for him by a few octaves.

There was Angela, the wannabe Army Cadet, with her do-it-yourself crew cut that made her look like Eric Cantona from the back. Her build was pretty similar too.

The list was varied and the stories were mostly funny ones now that he could look back on them, with the safety of hindsight.

Without realising the passage of time he had driven the almost twenty miles home, gone through the centre of his home town and was a few streets away from his small but comfortable one bedroom house which he was so proud to be able to say he owned - outright. No mortgage, no debts.

He parked his car. His head fell with the realization that he was in for yet another exchange with the mad old bat from over the road. She was already crossing the road towards him, he looked up, took a deep breath and smiled before undoing his seat belt and getting out of the car.

"I don't like to complain Mr Stapleton, I really

don't, but really, I just can't have this all the time."

The old woman was very strong of character and didn't mince her words when she got going but was always careful to start off very pleasantly, even going so far as seeing if she could get the other person to be first to say a heated word.

"And a good afternoon to you Miss West. I am in a hurry," Marcus said without letting her have any eye contact. She thrived on eye contact.

"Well I was in a hurry this morning too. Imagine how I felt having to see all of my beds scratched up like that. It is a disgrace. And I have spoken to you about it before."

"Miss West," he raised his voice slightly. "As I've said before I doubt very much that Casper would go around digging up your flower beds."

"Well who else?"

"I haven't a clue but I thought we'd agreed that if you see him doing it you have my permission to throw anything you have handy at him. That is how sure I am that Casper isn't to blame. Now if you don't mind..."

"Assaulting a pussy cat."

"Oh, for crying out loud..."

"I really don't think you take me seriously Mr Stapleton."

"If all you have to worry Miss West is the state of your second-rate flower beds then you are a very lucky woman indeed. Now if you'll excuse me."

"Just so you know, I have taken steps to make sure that it stops. I've put poison along the edging of the beds now. Any cat, yours or anyone other, that goes there is in danger of a very upset tummy. So unless you want sick all over your carpets and a vets bill through your door I suggest you control that animal."

"Casper is controlled Miss West," Marcus turned from her and fiddled to find his house key on a bunch of keys that needed sorting out. He added in thought not words that the only thing around here that was in danger of losing control was him as he pondered how best to get some of her poison into her own stomach.

"We'll see. You see if I'm not right..."

He entered the house and switched the hall light on.

There was a smell.

There was a split second pause of recognition. The smell was gas, but he realised it too late. Everything went white, then red. He was aware of intense pain as his ears shattered with an explosion that ripped half of the skin from his frame.

He wasn't aware of becoming airborne, or of landing and breaking every one of the bones that hadn't already been shattered in the explosion.

The fireball, which engulfed the house, rose in to a plume and then extinguished itself quite suddenly. Only the shape of the plume in smoke remained above the partly vaporized remains of the house.

Marcus's body was found by the emergency services across the road, smashed beyond recognition.

Miss West suffered a few broken bones but her injuries weren't life threatening. She became absolutely hysterical though when Casper the cat walked past her from the direction of her garden.

She had to be sedated.

PART TWO...

When Marcus woke he was in a hospital unable to move and unable to speak. He knew there were people around him but no one seemed to even know he was there.

After the initial panic of where he was and why he was there he managed to get some of his thoughts together to try to piece together in his own mind what had happened. As he tried to calm his thoughts down he became more aware of his surroundings and of himself and slowly memory flashes returned to him.

He saw his house, the fire, the noise reverberated around inside his head, yet he wasn't in pain. Surely he should be able to feel something.

He was flying through the air, the fire moving away from him, but the heat was unbearable, he could feel the skin erupting in blisters as it boiled, he thudded in to the ground. Why couldn't he feel something?

His memories started to come back quicker, less clearly, the lights, blue lights flashing continuously. Couldn't someone switch the damn things off?

The noise of sirens. Shouting. Screams.

Miss West was screaming, shouting and ranting like a mad woman. He assumed she too had been caught in the ferocious blast.

He saw a gas-company van drive up and realised what must have happened.

He'd never liked gas and so had always been cautious around it. He would think twice about having the stuff at all in future.

When he tried to move, he expected to feel pain shoot to his every extremity, but instead he found himself totally numb of all sensation and quite unable to move anything. Even his eyeballs seemed reluctant to move and seemed to move less when he wanted them to, but more when they wanted to.

He could hear voices getting nearer. Suddenly people were passing him, yet no one gave him any attention for some time.

A woman arrived in green scrubs and started to push the bed he was on through some corridors, he couldn't understand how the hospital was so quiet.

"Another one for me...? Jesus, where the hell's he come from?" a second woman he couldn't see said, he guessed from the other side of the room.

He felt nothing, no sensation at all but his eyes gave him the information he needed. He was lifted up off the bed, on to another bed.

"Explosion a few hours ago," the first woman replied. "Quite a mess."

Marcus was starting to get angry at being ignored so plainly to his face, yet still there was no control over his mouth, he couldn't speak.

There was a clatter of metal on metal, overhead lights came on, "You assisting?"

The first woman replied that she was.

He lunged into a torrent of silent screams and unmoving frantic tosses and turns in search of freedom as a scalpel came in to view and an autopsy began.

PART THREE...

Marcus watched what was not easily recognizable as his body, being cut, opened, examined and dissected. Parts were liquefied in a very kitchen-type of blender and the dark red goo transferred to slides. The gory process continued for what seemed like hours. He was insulted at the apparent small size of his brain, the lack of mention of the size of other parts of his body and the fact that he was diagnosed quite wrongly as having been a heavy drinker based on a very cursory seeming examination of his liver.

At first he hadn't thought it odd that he was somewhere other than in his own body. When he realised it, he found it amazing and the sights before him totally mesmerizing. Even the horror of the situation was muted from somewhere inside that he couldn't possibly understand.

After it was all over he saw his remains being sewn up so as the body remained in one piece (even though to his disgust several pieces were now missing) and then transferred to a refrigerated cabinet.

As that door closed he was suddenly aware of sensation. It came to him like a blow to the head, first he was falling. Everything faded from sight and then, suddenly he was standing. It was sunny. He recognized where he was straight away. The front at Southsea: he'd been here three times as a child, every time disappointed that the beach was covered with pebbles rather than sand.

He absorbed the view for moment, the sea was half way out, there were no boats, he loved looking out to sea and seeing boats. The huge oil tankers slowly slipping their way across the horizon were a fixation since childhood.

Then it struck him.

Amidst all that he could see and hear he was totally alone. There were no people, no cars, no busses, there were no birds. He looked around him, time and time again, sure that eventually he would see or hear something. Then he realised that he wasn't just hearing the absence of people, birds and traffic. He couldn't hear anything.

He ran to the end of the walk he was on, and leapt over the railings on to the pebbles, running towards the sea.

He ran but came to a jarring halt.

He trod heavily. Even the pebbles under foot made no sound. He nervously approached the sea and again, there was no sound. No sound of water. No sound of waves.

He could hear absolute silence in the presence of the sea.

He fell to his knees; despair tugged at him, his mind must be playing tricks. He thought about it as calmly as he could and concluded he must be sedated, or unconscious because of the explosion maybe. The whole thing, being in hospital, the morgue... Being here and seeing this... All must be a trick of the mind, trying to protect him from the injuries and horror of the real world.

He stood up and movement caught his eyes, he always had good peripheral vision.

A man was stood on the front, a few hundred metres away.

Marcus paused, looked again, checking his vision.

The figure turned and started to walk away.

Elated, Marcus ran. Hindered by the pebbles at first but he ran for his life. As he got up on to where the figure had been, he found himself alone.

He ran in the direction it had been, headed toward a small group of buildings that turned out to be public toilets and paused. The man couldn't have just disappeared so he hesitantly stepped towards the toilets.

As his foot came down on the floor of the inside of the toilet building he felt something soft under foot. He looked down. He was stood in deep grass, as he looked up he found himself on a windswept mountainside.

Dumfounded, he fell to the floor and sat and waited in confusion for his mind to sort something out for him, for right now, he had nothing. Knew nothing, understood nothing.

As he looked up the clouds raced, day turned to night, a half-moon arced across the sky as if by some science fiction style special effect in seconds and the sun rose again. Wind rose and fell, then something else happened. Marcus slowly rose to his feet and waited for the strength to turn to face whomever it was that he was so sure was stood a short distance away.

He was face to face with himself as he turned, the surprise, fright even, knocked him so much that he almost fell.

He stepped back in shock and as steps became less and less firm he found a clump of grass too much to navigate and he was on his backside.

He was on his backside in a shallow pool in a hotel in New Zealand. He'd stayed there for a few days while journeying around the country for a month. It had been an 'experience' holiday from his parents to celebrate his twenty-first birthday.

"Have you seen enough to talk or do you need to see more," his other-self asked.

He looked around but saw no one.

In fear he dared not speak so got slowly to his feet and once again looked around him.

"This should be a two-way process," the voice said.

"Am I unconscious, drugged?" he shouted.

"You aren't drugged and no, not unconscious."

"Then what the hell's…?"

"It's time," the voice was at his shoulder, he was startled turned and looked himself in the eye. "Time to talk, to see and for you, to listen."

"Are you me? You look like me, sound like me..."

"I have a question for you."

"I want answers not questions."

"I will ask questions and you will provide answers to both mine and your questions."

"And if I tell you to pi..." the mirror image of himself was gone.

"You don't get to decide what happens here," the voice said loftily from all around him. "Let's see what is ahead. Firstly to your school. Then to your office and, well, then maybe we'll visit... Well we'll see."

"Is this some kind of new-age hippie Christmas Carol style brain washing technique or something...?" he was stood in the sports hall of his old school surrounded by school children running in relays from one end to the other.

"Spot yourself?" the mirror image of him asked, once again having arrived at his shoulder.

Marcus was looking at himself as a child, but said nothing.

"Were you the first thing you looked for?"

"What if I was?" Marcus asked, walking off in to the sports hall to where his younger self was catching his breath before his next dash.

"Your first instinct was to look for yourself. What does this tell you about you, Marcus?"

"That I wanted to see what I was like back then," he replied, waving his hands around in front of the assembled children. He didn't ask the obvious.

"Do you remember the dark-haired lad?"

"No," Marcus looked at the boy. "Oh don't tell me, he was really the ghost of Christmas Present in disguise trying to work out whether or not I get to carry chains around with me in the afterlife..."

An icy wind filled the hall but only Marcus felt it, it shivered him to his spine. "You're not too far from the truth there Marcus. Perhaps if you'd thought less selfishly all these years, helped a few people out, this conversation would have ended already. Perhaps if you'd been a friend to him," the mirror image Marcus pointed to the dark haired boy wearing creased gym clothes, waiting quietly and nervously for his next turn to run. "His name is Carl. Pleasant lad, never said an unkind word to anyone the whole time he was in school. Had a few unkind thoughts about some of his classmates but only to be expected. You remember this...?"

The young Marcus did his run. He kept good time all the way down the hall, crashed in to the wall a little at the other end, turned quickly and sprinted back. He handed the baton to Carl who strode off and made up the small amount of time necessary to keep their team from losing their first place.

"That's the only heat your team won. Carl did good there, don't you think?"

"Yes. And there I am giving him a pat on the back. I think I kind of remember him a bit."

"That was the first day you'd spoken to him. You'd been in the same year together for two years, yet you never even said 'Hi'."

"So I was a shy child."

Marcus's body started to tremble, light built up inside him and started to streak towards Carl. In seconds, a transfer was complete.

"I want you to feel what Carl felt that day."

Marcus was paralysed, fear mainly stopping him from shrieking out at what was being forced upon him.

He watched from behind the eyes of Carl as his younger self came towards him, and said "Well done. We really needed that sprint of yours at the end." And then walked into the changing room.

The trembling sensation returned, lights flashing and streaking across the room to his own form.

"It felt wonderful didn't it?"

"You scared the... What is going here?"

"When you were Carl, when you saw your younger self coming towards you. What did that feel like? Good?"

Marcus nodded.

"And when he spoke to you, something that

wasn't an insult. How did that feel?"

Marcus was forced to think for a moment. He was stumped at the realization that he'd actually felt the sensations of that boy. The sheer joy, at something so simple as a friendly word. A friendly word and a feeling of belonging that had been within his power to bestow.

The whole room transformed in to a hallway in the school, Marcus could see himself in a line of other children waiting to be allowed in to one of the science labs. Carl was walking up the corridor and joined the line, two kids away from the young Marcus.

Marcus looked over to his mirror image as he felt the trembling sensation start once again. In moments he was inside Carl once again. There was relief at the sight of a friendly face, he smiled slightly at the young Marcus but there was no smile in return, the young boy turned his back to him and started talking to one of his friends. The sense of desolation was totally unexpected then the trembling returned and he was once again the adult Marcus.

"Not so good that time."

Marcus took a deep breath and then straightened himself up. "What's this supposed to achieve? You showing me that I was a normal fickle child? Well, yes I was. Like every other child I was a child, with all my faults, flaws, selfishness, the complete package. Are we done?"

"The question is: Do I now have your attention?"

"I think you can be pretty sure that you had my attention when I saw a night pass in seconds.

When I saw myself being in a lab, or maybe even when I was flying through the sky with a gas explosion for an enema and half of my face trying to mate with my left ear."

"So much anger. One would have thought by now the time had come for you to grow up Marcus...

Marcus was sat at a table in a dining room surrounded by people. There was laughter, drinking, and music playing. "Annette's leaving do..." he said, shocked.

"You remember this?"

"It was the first office party I went to," he said sheepishly, he paused nervously. "Why am I here?"

"Why are 'we' here? You do have a self-importance thing going on don't you?"

"As far as I'm concerned..."

"Which to you is all that matters."

"As far as I'm concerned you are a figment of my imagination. A shock induced hallucination, or a drug induced one. You're not even here. So 'I', 'I', 'I' bloody 'I'... You can either like it or else piss the hell off out of my head."

The mirror of himself vanished, then he too was somewhere else. At the side of a road, traffic passing by oblivious to these two observers.

"Your second car."

Marcus knew the road and was nervous already, the memory was in his head.

"You drove like a fool and one day..." he pointed as a blue car approached, faster than it should.

"No," Marcus shouted. He closed his eyes.

A dog ran out in to the road, the car hit it.

There were sounds. A thump, a screaming yelp of the animal and the screech of tyres, but the car didn't stop.

In a blurred flash the scene reset.

Marcus looked and saw no trace of the dog.

His frame trembled, lights streaked out of his body and then he was aware of being close to the ground, sniffing with an intensity that blew his mind away. He heard something, a screaming whistle and then he was running.

He was on tarmac, under a wheel and then left, alone, dying. It all happened so quickly and yet at the same time seemed to happen in slow motion.

Marcus was returned to his own body.

He flew at the mirror of himself in rage and fell straight through him.

"Speak to me like that again and I will make you experience the pain and suffering of every ant you ever trod on, every fly you ever swatted, every spider squashed and anything and everything else you have ever caused any harm to in anyway. Do we understand each other?"

Shaken, angry enough to rip a man limb from limb, Marcus conceded the unearthly superiority of this reflection of himself and waited.

After a few moments they were both back at the office party.

"Is this really necessary?" Marcus asked. "Can't I just wake up?"

"You are not asleep."

"I must be."

"No. Try pinching yourself, punching yourself, shouting, whatever. You'll find that you can't wake, not from this."

"Are you real?" Marcus asked with dread of any answer. Both 'yes' and 'no' seemed to hold a certain degree of insanity to them.

"The only thing in any of this that is real, is you. Everything is of you. And yes that includes me."

Marcus was dumfounded and failed to ask anything, his attempts at words were incomprehensible.

"My little reaction with the dog. That was how you would have reacted in my place. If you were angry with me then you were and are angry with yourself."

"None of this makes any sense." He looked around him then harder at his mirror image, "The explosion, did that really happened? The hospital, the morgue… All real?"

"In every sense that you mean, yes they were real."

"I'm...? I mean, you know... You mean..."

"That you're dead?"

"Am I?"

"In every sense that you mean, yes."

"And I'm in Hell being tortured by myself? Is that what this is?"

"Marcus, I thought after all this time you'd get this far quicker. This isn't hell. This is nothing like hell."

"Thank God for... I'm sorry," he looked up, "I didn't mean that." He looked back to his other self, "I mean I'm glad it's not."

There was a pause, it was eerie. "Am I going to go to hell?" he asked very slowly.

"Marcus, this place is your reprieve. This is the

place you come to and where I check that everything is as it should be."

"Reprieve? From...?"

"You have lived six hundred and sixty six lives and now it is time to see that you haven't become a more pleasant understanding creature than ever you were."

"Six hundred and sixty six," Marcus said slowly, near silently.

"Averaging sixty years a throw, that's thirty nine thousand nine hundred and sixty years of living give or take a few. Of course you don't survive birth every time... Even get flushed occasionally... When you do survive... You might die as a child, or young adult. Mostly though you do tend to get in to the higher figures. You always were quite good at self-preservation."

The words weren't being heard.

"6-6-6" Marcus thought out loud. "As in 6-6-6?"

His question was greeted with a knowing nod.

"But that's..."

"Your very own identity badge."

"Reprieve? Reprieve from what?"

"You are sentenced to what in your terms you call hell. To us, it is the sentence of life. Of living. You will endure the living hell and live another six hundred and sixty lives before once again you will be reviewed."

Marcus was shaking from fright. "You mean everyone is actually in hell when they're alive. Earth is the punishment from somewhere else?"

"No Marcus. You are all that truly exists, all that has ever existed there."

Marcus said nothing.

"You are the sole occupant of hell. You are the only being that 'lives', all else is a figment of your imagination. All the things you've done, places you've been, things you've seen. Ironically, you never actually did anything or ever went anywhere. You are all that you know of that truly exists. And let's face it, the world that you create around you is predictably illustrative of your character. A world of hardship, of want, a world of war between countries, famine affecting the weakest and greed absorbing the strongest… I've seen and heard enough…"

His mirror image disappeared before his eyes.

He was aware of immense sensation once again, the feeling of falling, then rising, the falling… The sensations repeated themselves over and over until suddenly without warning he was floating. There was a rhythmic near silence. Warmth. A comfortable darkness.

He remained like that for a while, his mind racing but still aware of so much.

Then there was movement, sudden, jerking, powerful movement.

Light erupted from every angle.

After what could have been minutes, or months, he couldn't tell, he was aware of pressure on the sides of his head, a pulling sensation and then…

He was born again.

He spent some time screaming his objections, shouting for help. But all around him was as he would have expected, for a delivery room. No one understood the screaming baby. The futility of his situation dawned eventually, not long before all of his memories of who he was and why he was there started to become more and more of a blur.

His sentence started once again.

Life number one...

MICHAEL EWERS

REUNION

Tom...

May the 3rd had not been kind to Tom so far and it was only mid-afternoon. He'd learnt the hard way that success was a cross to bear and he bore it all the time. There were high spots of course, but they tended to be fleeting. Right now he was sat comfortably in a nearly new Ford, the car of his choice; he could afford it...for now. The comfort though was lost on him. His neck ached as it tended to do most days, his back twinged every time he leant forward and round to check over his shoulder before overtaking and his eyes were tired. All this by two twenty he thought to himself as he checked the clock.

The M4 motorway wasn't as busy as he'd feared it might be a pleasant surprise that was ruined by the heavy and persistent rain that restricted the speed of traffic. His tension levels rose as he switched the CD player off for a while, fed up of the thing jumping every time the car went over the slightest bump in the road. He cursed to himself, the aerial was down and he couldn't stop for a while to put it up and even if he did he'd get soaked. He tried to enjoy some quiet for a while, a chance to think.

He was being hounded by his agent for the next couple of lines that he was assigned to produce, technically he was behind schedule but everyone knew the schedule had a wide safety margin built in for just these kinds of circumstances. Hell, if the damned greasy butter substitute couldn't sell based on taste what the difference was a catchy tune going to make?

He'd spent all morning listening to other people's opinions about the sort of music that tended to hold the attention of the audience. Apparently anything with too many high notes over more than four seconds was a turn off, too many low notes was just a turn over, not ideal for commercial television. These people talked such crap, and got paid even more than he did, for doing so. Then the client wanted to 'suggest' a few tag words that if included in the jingle would be 'absolutely marvellous'. They wanted 'buttery', 'creamy' or something similar... In their dreams. If possible there should be some reference to 'wholesome' and/or 'goodness', preferably both and if it could be arranged there should be mention of the products' competitive pricing. In short they wanted the best jingle for the least money, with a load of stupid words, a catchy tune and all right now. The answer had been, "Of course we will do what we can and present you with a few options by the end of the week." Fat chance.

Now, in the silence of the car, he should have

been able to try to come up with a few words that would string together, not a whole sentence, just something he could call a start.

Within minutes the CD player was back on and Cher was screeching to the best of her limited ability, anything to conceal the now unbearable creaks and groans coming from the car every time it went over a bump. Amazing though it may seem, this car went clonk over small bumps. There was a double clonk, that sounded more like a clonk-clenk, when it went over a large bump and if there was a full ditch there would be a clonk, a cleck, a clank and a few creeks from the back.

As he got nearer and nearer to Wales it got worse. Going over the Second Severn Crossing was like having a wannabee rap band on speed strapped to the underneath of the car that just wouldn't shut the hell up.

He just knew his blood pressure was rising.

He was putting himself through this all because of a stupid school reunion that he really didn't want to go to anyway.

Jane & Adam...

For Jane, tonight was the night she got to make an entrance. The entrance she'd wanted for as long as she could remember. The entrance she'd only been able, or secure enough, to try since halving her weight just a couple of years ago.

Her new dress was quite understated, black, with minimal accessories, she wanted people to see her, not what she was wearing. The makeup was almost applied and still, with less than two hours before the thing was due to start and a half an hour drive ahead of them, Adam wasn't home. He had ten more minutes she promised herself then she'd ring the office and find out where he was and shout obscenities at him to embarrass him in front of his colleagues. If he ruined her night that was the least he could expect.

The door went, she sighed. 'At last', she thought, then ran to the top of the stairs and told him not to bother doing anything else, just come up stairs, shower, get dressed and be ready to go in half an hour. That gave a little more time just in case he couldn't tie his tie, find his socks or insisted on a snack before leaving.

He obediently obeyed, didn't say too much, "Hi dear. Sorry I'm a little late," or words to that effect. She hadn't heard them, had no interest in hearing them.

While she applied her mascara he sat on the edge of the bed and stripped off.

The shower was a welcome relief to the stuffy office and the damp of the car. The heater was playing up again so in the rain he had had to struggle to drive and keep wiping the window clear of misting up.

He turned the shower up hotter than usual and massaged his neck a little. But for the sound of the water, the silence was bliss: he knew it couldn't last. He was going to have to stand beside his constantly preening wife for a good three or so hours this evening, a fate worse than eternal damnation in his mind. He sighed, it never used to be like that.

He stepped out of the shower, towel dried his hair, put on a bathrobe and walked, purposely quietly, in to the bedroom. If he was quiet he might not wake the monster.

"Finished at last?" she asked, her gaze fixed on her own reflection in the mirror.

Too late, she was awake.

"I was sticky, sweaty. Really needed that," he replied, trying to make the words and tone as neutral as possible.

"Not to mention stinking of smoke. Your clothes are at the bottom of the stairs."

She paused, perhaps that was all there would be for now, but then she took a deep breath, he knew there was more to come. "I suppose that means you saw Anderson today?"

"He is an important client..."

"All the same, he shouldn't smoke in your office... It is your office after all. You do have a say. My God, it's just common courtesy."

She carried on for a while. The mouth moved from first to second then third, fourth and finally fifth gear... She was on a roll.

He waited until she paused, not for breath mind, she never seemed to need that, but to gather her thoughts ready for round two.

"We'll need to take your car tonight," he told her, hoping to knock her off her chosen subject on to one she was less prepared for.

"Oh of course. I mean that's typical. The biggest night of the year for me and we can't take your car we have to take my little run around. They'll all be looking and feeling sorry for poor old Jane... I can just hear them 'She's only got a little 205'. They, of course will all be driving up in their flashy BMW's..."

"If you want a different car..."

"Don't you get funny with me. You know I can't see over the steering wheel of these big cars. Don't you dare got funny with me tonight. Tonight of all nights." She stomped off, stamped her way down the stairs and thankfully allowed a few moments of bliss to just happen. Well that was how it felt.

Kathy...

Great care was taken, her steps down the stairs were silent. She just knew they were. There was no way on this Earth that any human could have heard her but somehow her radar endowed mother managed and was at the bottom of the stairs to meet her. And how did she move so damned fast anyway for someone with a dodgy hip?

"Oh, you do look smart dear."

"Thanks mum," Kathy said, looking over her mother's shoulder to the full- length mirror. "You don't think it's a bit boring looking?" She edged sideways to get a better view of herself.

"Now you come here," her mother pulled her close and hugged her. "You look wonderful and are going to have a great time." They separated. "You never know, you might meet 'Mr Right' tonight."

"Oh, I doubt that Mum." Kathy knew that that was a physical impossibility.

"Don't you doubt yourself. You have it in you. You are beautiful. I don't understand how you're still single. Legs like that, perfect skin... the whole package. Model-material. I've always said you should have been a model..." Here we go again Kathy thought and managed to cut her mother off with a simple subject-changing question.

"How long should the taxi be?"

"The woman said 6:30, and it's only a ten minute drive, so don't fret if it's a few minutes late."

"I'm not fretting," Kathy said under her breath. "Just suffocating," she added silently.

She'd been home since yesterday. She thought it would be a bit much to expect to stay at her mother's just for the night of the reunion, so agreed with herself after some argument that she should put herself through a day with her mother both before and after the event. She would head back tomorrow evening if she lived that long... If her mother lived that long.

Paul (and Simon)...

In a casual suit, Paul did look good, Simon had said so before but not tonight. He couldn't, wouldn't, say so tonight.

He'd tried his best for over a week not to mention tonight. It was his hope not to give the slightest impression to Simon that he was just a little excited about the chance to go and meet up with some old friends from school. Arriving one day out of the blue, the letter about the reunion had brought home to him the fact that it was almost five years since they'd all seen each other, as a group anyway. He'd seen Kathy in the area a couple of times, once or twice they'd even stopped to exchange a few pleasantries, but they'd never really got on brilliantly in the past so a distant casual acknowledgment of each other was what seemed to work for the both of them. Perhaps more so for Paul than he'd dare admit, though Simon would have pounced on it in a second and given him plenty of grief over it.

As for Tom, Jane, Adam and Kevin, the others that made up their seemingly indestructible group (indestructible while they went through school at least), he'd seen none of them since the wedding. Almost five years.

Correction, he'd met Tom once at a party in Bristol and they got on fine, picking up pretty much as they left off. It was as if they'd only been separated by a day, rather than years. He'd picked up on a bit of gossip apparently Jane and Adam had a blissful marriage until the 'problem' of children came up. From what little Tom had gathered from two telephone conversations with Adam, spanning over a year, they were having difficulties because they both wanted children. Paul had quite a disarming way about him and had managed to get Tom to reveal that Jane had been ill years before and the advice she was given was that she should think very carefully about ever trying to have children as it could present a risk to her life. After much advice seeking and soul searching they decided to try for one child, but after months of very enjoyable 'trying' Adam was told that he had a very low sperm count.

The double whammy had ended their sex life, turned their conversations in to confrontations and their marriage of bliss in to an unfulfilling living arrangement.

There was so much about these people, so much that as a group they had shared. The walks, fun, games, hobbies, holidays, even a few accidents that he so wanted to tell Simon. But Simon would see through him and discover the lie and that was something he found so hard to deal with.

Yesterday though, that was all turned on its' head by a dream about the reunion and an almost over-whelming sense of 'what-the-hell'. He thanked god that Simon had already got up and gone to work when he himself woke or else he might have made an arrangement that he might not now be able to go through with.

He stood in the living room, silent behind the seat Simon was sat in, not quite sure whether Simon knew he was there. He waited, watching Simon sit there flicking through his favourite magazine, pausing briefly at a couple of the pictures, obviously not impressed with certain others. Paul grinned, they had the same taste.

Paul walked across to what was usually referred to as his chair and sat. There was silence, Simon didn't even look up. As if he didn't already know it, Paul got the clear message that he was hurting Simon. He knew of a possible solution, but would the risk of losing his friends, even if they were friends at a distance, too high a price for keeping his Simon?

Kevin...

Kevin had always been the 'Mr Sensible' of the group and today had the bizarre honour of being partly responsible for organizing the school reunion that all his old friends, classmates, some teachers and no doubt a few people he didn't want to ever see again, would be attending. The bizarre bit was that he was now one of the teachers at the very same school.

Unlike everyone else, he had grown to know the school throughout the little changes that had occurred over the last ten years. He wouldn't be surprised by the play-school-like paint job that the main building had been given or impressed by the new very professional looking lighting rig that spanned the stage in the main hall where everyone was soon to gather. He'd come to know the teachers at the school as colleagues, and in a few cases even regarded some of them as friends - something that would have been a nightmare scenario all those years ago.

The clock was ticking.

Food and refreshments were in place the seating was spread out to look informal, there was even a small disco set up that he dreaded being forced to perform in front of. Being the colleague to these people and yet one of the students being reunited was giving a slightly schizophrenic outlook on the whole event. To say he was in two minds was being hopeful, he was in fact swaying from manic to hysterical as he noticed the time ebbing away and the teachers arriving. Why did they have to do that anyway? Why did the teachers have to arrive early? Couldn't they do as the rest of the guests and turn up at the right time? No of course not. As teachers they wanted to check things out first, get comfortable, pick all the best seats and watch everyone arrive and give the judgment on them to anyone unfortunate enough to be close.

There would be a far more exaggerated case of what had been going around the staff room for weeks now. The comments about:

"You know so 'n so, well I used to teach her."

"That guy who props the bar up in 'Eastenders', almost every episode? He was my star drama student."

"Have you heard about this... Have you heard about that... About what he's doing...? Blaa blaa blaa."

For educators their conversation was lacking.

Kevin had given serious thought about not being here tonight. But it would seem very odd indeed, more so to the staff than to the ex-students and it would be very difficult to explain. There had been a lot of notice, a few months before the invitations were sent. He was pretty much stuck with it. But that was his outlook on life these days. Stuck with trying to teach biology to a bunch of dick-heads who's only concept of biology is the size of their breasts and when they'll get bigger in the case of the girls and what's going on between their legs in the case of the boys... Mind you, watching some of them during break times and when they're walking out of school sometimes it seems as if the topics overlap considerably.

Stood at the back of the hall, in front of huge windows, Kevin was stirred from his mental moaning about the shortcomings of his life by the arrival of several cars. They disappeared behind the sports-hall building for a few moments and then reappeared in the car park. His stomach churned.

Guests.

The Reunion...

There was a broad set of steps to climb before getting to the foyer that leads to the main hall. From the large windows spanning the rear of the hall all of the approaching guests could be seen and most of them were being identified by the assembled teachers and one or two ex-students.

Kevin heard the name Paul, a few seconds later it was linked with the surname Mason and he headed immediately towards the doors.

The current and ex-Headmasters were positioned by the doors to greet everyone as they arrived, Paul discreetly positioned himself where he could check whether it was indeed Paul, an old friend he hadn't seen for years, or someone else.

He recognized him immediately, walked straight up to him and offered his hand, but Paul was Paul and ever so slightly camp hugs were more his thing. They exchanged pleasantries and then stepped off to the side where Kevin could hide in plain sight using Paul for cover.

Their conversation covered nothing too deep and meaningful but for Paul it was tense, this was one of the friends he stood to possibly lose and as he talked to him, looked him in the eye, remembered the things of years gone by it suddenly seemed like a price too high. Always such a risk.

"Oh...my...God..." Paul stumbled for his words, his tongue falling over his lips... "Isn't that Jane?"

Kevin turned to see Jane and Adam being fawned over by the old headmaster.

"It might be half of her," Kevin commented.

"Tell me about it. She used to be twice that

size," Paul said, stating the obvious, but these words needed to be said.

As they stepped through the doors Jane and Adam were intercepted by Mrs James, she'd just been to pick up a glass of wine when she recognized Jane. Remarkably this old woman with very strong looking glasses recognized this transformed woman instantly. Jane was stuck for a while but after less than a minute Adam managed to excuse himself after catching sight of Kevin and Paul.

More pleasantries, more light conversation.

"Of course you realize I'll leave you high and dry when you get cornered by Miss Willis," Jane said acidly but with a broad smile as she arrived to join their group a few minutes later. "Paul," she hugged and kissed... "Kevin," she hugged and kissed. "Well, perhaps tonight won't be so bad after all. So what do you think of the new look?" She gave them a twirl, they both clapped briefly with approval. "You like?" she asked, fishing for comment, compliments and flattery.

They both fought for their words.

"I think that's a yes," Adam said on their behalf.

"I guess so," she leaned in close to her husband. "Shame I can't leave you lost for words from time to time." Kevin and Paul exchanged nervous glances.

"Oh, look. There's Jenny," Jane ran off, if you can call it running in four inch stiletto heels, to meet a girl she'd know years ago but never liked. She would enjoy flaunting her new look.

*

Kathy's arrival was little late thanks to her taxi and a driver who could take lessons from a homing pigeon and, as a result was a little low key. She even managed to avoid the wrinkly duo at the door.

She made her way quietly through the hall.

Nothing seemed to her to have changed. She walked through masses of people, apparently unnoticed until she spotted a familiar profile at a table, obviously a man being very indecisive over a choice of drink. Even that seemed familiar.

She leaned close and whispered, "White is usually a safe bet," she said quietly.

Adam straightened up but didn't turn around, "That's got to be Kathy." He turned, "Hello you. Wow, you're looking great. How are you?"

She looked around her nervously, "Intimidated?"

"Don't be. There's nothing in here good enough to intimidate anyone. Give me your arm," he put his arm through hers. "White is it?"

"Not for me thanks, I'll have something later." He picked up one for himself, "Paul and Kevin are just over there. We've been going over a few old times."

*

As the evening plodded on, the group each met up in various combinations, but one conspicuous absentee was Tom.

Jane had come to his defence, if any be needed, explaining that he was very successful at what he's been doing and just might have been unable to attend. No one thought too much of the fact he wasn't there because everyone knew from years ago about his way of working. When he's set on doing something his mind shifts a gear and the whole world ceases to exist for a while, just long enough for him to devote every ounce of his strength to the task at hand. Of all of them, he was the most likely to simply forget about the reunion under the pressure of work.

Over an hour in to the evening, with one end of the hall now dedicated to a disco and the conversation starting to get more difficult or in some cases a lot more serious, Kevin wandered the halls of the main building. He needed a break and some air, and got this with the excuse of needing to see to a call of nature. He thought it odd when, just as he was about to leave the second floor, he noticed at the far end of the corridor one of the biology lab lights was on.

There should be no one up here at all really, certainly not in any of the classrooms or labs. Assuming that someone had just left a light on by accident he went to switch it off.

When he opened the door he found it to be a lamp on one of the side-benches towards the back that was on.

"Kevin," he heard as he took his first step in to the lab. He froze.

"Who's in here?"

"It's me Tom."

"What are you doing in here?" he turned to put the main lights on.

"No don't please. I've got the most unbelievable migraine. Darkness is best," Tom explained.

"How long have you been in here?"

"Not long. Just as I was coming in I heard the music and thought I'd better try to get rid of this," he tapped his head "first. Noise, lights, conversation would just make me worse."

Walking up towards the back of the lab Kevin tried to get a view of Tom who was sat just forward of the light from the lamp, leaving his face in darkness. "Do you want me to take you home...I mean to where you're staying?"

"No, I'll be fine in a little while. I've taken medication, just need to let it do the job. It's probably just because I've been driving for hours. Most of the way it was raining so I really had to concentrate on the road."

"Well, can I get you anything? Drink, there's food in the hall..."

"A little conversation would be nice. I haven't spoken to anyone since about one this afternoon, unless you count swearing at the car."

Kevin pulled a stool out from under one of the benches and sat down, he was on the opposite side of the workbench Tom was sat at and yet couldn't properly make out his features. "So, feeling shitty aside, how are you doing?"

"As the saying goes, 'Life is like a box of chocolates...'

"'...You never know what you're going to get'. I saw that film too."

"When you think things are down, hopefully, fate gives you and hand up. And vice versa. But I know all about my problems. What about yours? Why are you in this dump when you should be doing your children's' books?"

"How do you know about that?"

"Because one of the companies you contacted years ago has your name on their filing system. Now answer the question."

Kevin thought for a moment, "It takes time and backing for that sort of thing. And I'm not convinced I have anything different enough to fend off the competition. Of which by the way there is a lot."

"You know Kevin if you don't trust in yourself, no one else ever will."

"It's not that simple..."

*

Outside the main hall, down the steps and round the other side of a group of fir trees, Adam and Paul were sat on a wall both lighting up cigarettes.

"If Jane knew I'd started smoking she'd shove this up my arse. Lighted end first." Adam took his first pull and savoured the experience.

"Want to tell me about you and Jane?" Paul asked.

"You know what's going on there Paul. We've drifted apart. The fine line between love and hate was crossed years ago and now we just barely manage tolerance."

"Does that mean you're going to split?"

"She's too much in love with the married lifestyle, with being married. I am just as bad, can't bear the thought of not having someone to come home to. Even if she is a banshee." Another, longer draw on the cigarette.

"You're afraid of being alone. Damn good reason. I'd say most people are afraid of being alone, especially as they get older."

They sat for a moment, "I don't know how you cope with it."

Paul felt the muscles in his stomach tense, the words came out without any control, "I'm not on my own."

It was Adam's turn to feel tense, he said what his gut had been wanting to say since they were in school, "So what's his name?"

They were both locked into looking forward. Each took some thinking time in the form of another suck on their cigarettes.

"It is a 'him', right?"

"Simon," Paul said, quietly.

"I feel," he looked for the right word, "saddened, that you didn't feel able to bring him here tonight. You really should have."

"Does this change anything?" Paul asked hesitantly.

"No. Hell, I've... Well I haven't ever 'been' with a man, but I can appreciate the attraction. I kissed Colin Robson once in the changing rooms down there," he pointed to the sports hall building in front of them.

"You're kidding!"

"No I'm not."

"But he's here isn't he?"

"He is and is looking as good as ever he did in school, even if he is going thin on top."

Paul was falling over his thoughts, he had little chance at words, "How? When? I mean, crikey, say something."

"Do you remember when he had his broken arm? Well, he was off P.E. and I'd just had to have an operation on my eye so I was off too and you know what Mr Black was like: total bastard when it came to not doing sports. So we were locked in the changing room for the best part of fifty minutes with two hundred lines to write. We talked about loads of stuff, were sat next to each other. After a little while it kind of just happened."

"How the hell can it just happen? Trust me Adam, I know when it comes to kissing guys, it does not 'just happen'. Didn't you think he was going to punch you in the face for trying it? How come he didn't think you'd punch him in the face for him trying it with him? Come to think of it, why didn't you?"

"Are you kidding? Colin Robson? I spent four years walking down to that football field behind him because of those legs. I prayed to be picked for the opposite side to him so that I could get in there, tackle him."

"Forgive me for asking this to a married man, but I feel the need: do you even know which team you are batting for?"

Adam flicked his almost extinct cigarette away, "I appreciate both teams. I just, don't feel able to live the life of your team. I've only ever been attracted to, maybe four or five men in my whole life, compared to hundreds of women."

There was a pause.

"Well come on, you can't leave it there. Anyone else I know? Anyone else from school?"

"From school?" Adam paused, a long pause this time. Then finally answered nervously, "Only you."

*

Kathy and Jane were touching up their make up in the ladies and had already discussed a range of subjects. They'd had plenty of time to do so while they peed.

"Sometimes I think life would be so much easier if I was a lesbian myself," Jane said.

For Kathy it was close to being the comment that caused her to lose control, she almost burst out in tears.

Confident that she hadn't said anything wrong, for she believed that she never did, Jane put her arm on Kathy's shoulder and insisted that she hear all about it.

The story was complex but suitably simplified for Jane. The first terrifying situation was that her mother was still living in her own blissful little world in which Kathy would soon meet the man of her dreams. Secondly was the fact that Kathy and her partner had both wanted a child so much that they arranged for Kathy to get impregnated. Jane couldn't help but ask the who's, how's etc and Kathy explained it was quite simple involving a cup, a 'deposit' and a syringe. The rest she left for Jane to piece together later. Thirdly was the fact that Kathy and her partner of over three years had split just before going through with the impregnation and finally, that Kathy had wanted a baby so much that she went through with it anyway.

The world-stopper was going to be how the hell to tell her mother that she was a pregnant lesbian and would not be meeting her ideal man no matter how much her mother prayed for it each night when she went to bed.

*

"Me?" Paul almost chocked on his lost lung full of toxic chemicals.

"Yup. Not in quite the same lustful way as I considered Colin, but yes. I always thought of you as a bit of all right. Always thought you batted for that team and I suppose I resented, a little bit, the fact that you would never confide in me. I hated the thought you might tell in someone else. At the time I thought maybe you didn't trust me enough with something that 'big', that important. Or maybe you thought I wouldn't be able to deal with it."

They both sat in thought for a while. Paul stood up, "Do you remember that summer we all went camping? I wished, I prayed, that Kevin wouldn't be able to come so that we could share a tent together. I settled for being able to sit next to you in geography for fifty minutes every Monday morning." Paul turned his back to Adam. "Used to make my week," he started to walk back to the main hall.

"Paul," Adam caught up with him and stood in front of him. "Wait. I want to say thank you, for telling me. And, to apologize for never telling you."

"What could have been, hey?"

"I'll make you a deal. If at our twentieth reunion we're both single, I'll ask you out on a date." Adam smiled. "In front of everyone."

"Now that I would like to see."

*

Close to tears herself, Jane explained to Kathy how her life had lost all sense of meaning after the discovery that between them she and Adam had very little chance of ever having children.

For the first time she spilled out the rage she felt towards Adam and the guilt she felt towards herself for feeling like that towards a man whom she knew all too well would give her the moon on a silver platter if he could. A man who loved her far more than perhaps she deserved.

"I suppose that is irony," Kathy accepted. "And the clock is ticking."

"Your mother will realise you know."

"I have to tell her tomorrow. I promised myself I would, but she's driving me crazy all the time. The talk of men, of husbands. You know, a few weeks ago I came to visit for the day and almost grabbed the dictionary to show her what the word lesbian means. She doesn't grasp it. It's in one ear round the mountains and out the other ear."

"It may just be her way of coping. Most of what Adam says to me these days goes straight in and out. That way I don't tend to find too many things to shout at him about."

"Perhaps that's good though."

"It's me being selfish, because it's less I'll have to feel guilty about afterwards."

*

As Paul and Adam came in to the foyer they met a beaming Kevin.

"You just had a bonk or are you on something?" Adam asked.

"Neither. I've just realised that teaching isn't for me, not anymore anyway. I swear I can actually physically feel the weight lifting off my shoulders. Feels absolutely amazing." Kevin looked at them both, he let out a long sigh, "I feel better than I have done in as long as I can remember."

"And you decided or realised, this why?" Paul asked.

"Tom. He's not feeling very well, bad head, chucking up a bit too I think..."

"Tom's here?"

"He's in biology lab two taking it quiet for a while. But I'm sure he'd like to see you," Kevin suggested. "I'm, I think, I think I'm going to go and have a dance." Kevin walked off with a never before seen spring in his step.

"I'm going to see Tom."

"Paul, before you do, are we okay? Really?"

"Adam, we're good. Yeah. Missed chances can hurt, but yes we are fine."

Adam ushered Paul to one side, "You know there's no guarantee that if we had shared a tent..."

"Take my word for it..."

"Are you saying I'm easy?" Adam suppressed a laugh not wanting to attract attention.

Paul whispered, "Adam, if we'd shared a tent and I knew then what I know now I would have given you the most amazing night of your life. Several times, with a bit of luck. I may not have been experienced back then but by god I was bloody willing."

Paul hugged Adam and for the first time he felt Adam hugging back.

It felt so good.

He felt so good.

They separated. "You've been working out," Paul said. "Suits you."

*

Paul and Tom had always got on very well together, but Paul always felt that their friendship had an air of tolerance about it. As if they were each tolerating each other because they wanted to be with everyone else in the group. They had never done anything together without others from their group being involved, until the last year of school.

In that last year, Tom had introduced Paul to a wide range of music that he'd never known existed and Paul had convinced Tom that he had a real talent for writing both lyrics and melody. Tom had gone on to use that talent successfully in his professional life and had done well for himself, while Paul had continued to explore music and learn an appreciation for it. He felt very grateful to Tom for opening his ears. In that last year they spent a great deal of time together and became the friends that neither of them had expected.

*

Jane was a little the worse for wear. She'd been drinking steadily and as usual it had gone straight to her head. For the last five minutes she'd been listening mostly to Mr Powell. He hadn't offered her a first name to call him by which she resented, going on about how the art department was expanding, explaining, how the youngsters these days seemed to have far more talent and how he as her old teacher was very disappointed that she hadn't kept up her drawing as she'd been so very good at it.

Jane hadn't endeared herself to him with her first reply about the talent of youngsters today being less about the ability to draw and paint but more about how even a big yellow splash of paint on an otherwise blank piece of paper was regarded as art these days and that, as a result just about anything was regarded as good by someone. Mr Powell had reddened considerably and at that point Jane settled in to listening mode and kept an eye out for someone or something that might enable her to escape. Where was Adam when she needed him most?

As her frustration grew, Adam appeared at her shoulder, he could tell from the look of the back of her that she was close to exploding but was maintaining her show of dignity. He thought about letting her stew for a little while longer but that wasn't really in his nature. "Jane dear, there you are," he leaned over her from behind and kissed her gently, "Paul and I have been waiting for you in the foyer."

Jane made her apologies to Mr Powell, Adam said hello to him but had never been taught by him so made no attempt at conversation.

As soon as they were out in the foyer Jane said what Adam had been sure she'd have said. He was surprised she managed to hold the comment back this long. "You stink of smoke." He covered by saying something about Paul smoking while he'd been talking to him and the two carried on.

Adam escorted Jane towards a flight of stairs, she continued to moan about how the speeches were soon to start and she'd thought she was going to have to endure Mr Powell and the speeches at the same time. They went up the stairs and on to the main corridor, "Are we supposed to be up here?"

Adam didn't reply, he carried on towards

biology lab two. She passed on the bit of gossip about Kathy being pregnant as they walked almost the full length of the building in this poorly lit central corridor.

When they entered the lab Paul was shouting another 'goodbye' to Tom and was coming out. "Hey, I was wondering about a quiet get-together? Any chance you two can make lunch tomorrow?" Paul asked.

"Certainly can," Jane replied. "Did you say Tom? Is that Tom in there?"

"Work's very busy..." Adam started to say but Jane cut him off. "You own the damn place. Take an hour off for dinner. I'm sure the staff won't think you've emigrated."

"The Gryphon at 12:30?" Paul suggested.

"We'll be there," Jane said firmly and stepped in to the lab.

"You okay?" Adam asked.

"Yeah. Tom and I have just had a chat. I think I'll take your and his advice."

"Really?"

"Wait and see," Paul started to walk away. "Oh," he ran the few paces back to Adam, "As, thanks to you, I am extremely horny I'm heading home now. For an early night," he smiled broadly. "I'll see you tomorrow. Can you let Kevin and Kathy know about tomorrow for me?"

*

When Jane and Adam came out of the biology lab they made their way to the main hall. As they were going in Kathy was pulling on her jacket to leave.

"Going already Kathy?" Jane asked.

"I'm feeling tired, and I do need to see mum tonight if possible. Catch her before she goes to bed."

"Paul's asked us to spread the word about lunch tomorrow. 12:30 at the Gryphon, you remember it? Will you be able to join us?" Adam asked. "It should be a bit quieter than this."

"I'll certainly try, as long as mum's got nothing planned for me," she looked at Jane, knowing that her plans for tomorrow depended on whether her mother threw a complete fit at hearing that her unmarried lesbian daughter was over two months pregnant.

Outside and strolling down the steps of the school, Kathy was glad of a cool breeze, some peace and quiet and the chance to drop the pretence of happiness she was wearing for the occasion.

She pulled out her mobile 'phone and called for a taxi, luckily she should only have to wait about ten minutes.

She walked around the car park for a few minutes. All of a sudden a car engine started up, lights came on and a car started to move towards her, she hadn't seen anyone else at all in the car park, she'd seen no one go to their car. It stopped when the driver's window was level with her, the window wound down.

"Kathy, hi."

She looked for a moment, "Tom?"

"It is indeed. Do you need a lift?"

"Well, if you'd asked a few minutes ago, but I've just ordered a taxi..."

Tom turned the car off and got out, "Then I'll

wait with you until it comes. So how are you? You're looking well... Almost glowing."

"Interesting choice of words..." her eyes filled up.

"Hey, have I said something wrong?"

"Oh Tom, I'm in a mess."

They got in to the car and Kathy explained as she'd done so to Jane earlier.

"Why do you think your mother is so eager to see you get married?" Tom asked.

Lunch...

The Gryphon, located a half a mile or so outside of the town, was close to where Kevin had lived as a child. As a result of this, it was a regular haunt for his family in years gone by, for himself and his friends as soon as they were old enough to go out to dinner without adult supervision and a year or two later it became their local as they each became old enough to move from coke to cider, wine, beer or whatever they fancied that had alcohol in it.

Ten years or so ago, it had been Tom out of their group that had had the last exam, everyone else was finished with their exams by a Wednesday, but Tom had one on the Thursday. It was the last Thursday any of them had spent in school and was the day that they all went out and celebrated in loud style.

Kevin was early: it was something of a character flaw for him. He'd slept far more soundly than he thought he would, waking up to feel truly refreshed and ready for the world. He'd done his usual thirty minutes on an exercise bike, showered, marked essays and for over an hour and then had breakfast. After a walk to a nearby supermarket for a few items he strolled home and set about writing the letter he'd had composed in his head for over two years. That done he was now waiting, nervously, for the next of the group to arrive.

Adam, Jane and Kathy arrived together, the former having apparently arranged last night to give the latter a lift. Kathy had become aware as quickly then as Kevin was now of the difference in the body language between Adam and Jane. They were holding hands and as they entered the inner set of doors Kevin could clearly see that they were smiling at each other like they used to. Almost lustful.

They all greeted each other and Adam set about ordering drinks. As he stepped up to the bar he met Paul who was walking closely beside a slightly taller man who even Adam had to agree was one hell of a hunk. Even with a casual suit on this guy was obviously what people had in mind when they said swimmers build. He wasn't sure whether he envied Paul or Simon the most for a moment but he came to his senses and allowed Paul to make his first, nervous introduction.

Adam and Simon shook hands, Adam and Paul gave each other a little hug and they all three then chatted about very little until the drinks were ready which they gathered up and transferred to the table where the others were sat.

"Everyone, I'd like to introduce Simon," Paul said, almost bluntly. "Simon is the man in my life. Simon, this is Jane, Adam's wife," he gestured, Simon leaned over to shake Jane's hand as she rose, she leaned in farther and gave him a peck on the cheek.

"A pleasure," she said warmly.

Paul continued, they each welcomed Simon as a friend without so much of a flinch of disapproval. Paul was amazed, almost euphoric, by the time he made the final introduction, to Kevin.

"For future reference Paul, and everyone else, when your boyfriend looks as good as that, you do not keep him a secret," Jane said, once again warmly, smiling broadly and hugging Adam's arm much to everyone else's unease.

Could this woman be on something she'd forgotten to take last night?

The drink went down quickly, everyone had news. They were all fidgeting, making nonsense talk not wanting to get to the good stuff until they were all together but by the time they'd finished their first drinks and were getting ready to move to the restaurant area, Tom still hadn't arrived.

As they took their seats, Jane could contain herself no longer and finally announced that she and Adam had some news. Something fantastic and she couldn't wait to tell them and Tom would understand... They all paused, Adam and Jane held hands and looked at each other, into each other's eyes - the picture of happiness. "We've spent the morning with the solicitor and we're getting divorced as soon as we can," she exploded with such glee it was as if she were announcing a multi-million pound lottery wins.

Everyone was silent.

Shouldn't this be devastating news?

They were all thinking the same thing but

saying nothing. No one knew what to say and no one was going to be first to say it.

"It makes so much sense now," Jane explained. "As soon as we could see beyond our own situation it was obvious that this was what we needed."

"We were up for hours last night. We talked and talked. Just like old times," he kissed Jane on the cheek. "We think too much of each other to make the other unhappy and that is what we are while we're together."

Still no one knew what to say. Paul finally plucked up the courage to say, "Congratulations," with painful hesitation.

Checking Adam and Jane's reaction first, everyone else chimed in with similar words of support.

"While we're all celebrating," Kathy said nervously, fighting a little to be heard, "I'd like to let you all know that I am pregnant."

Once again the congratulations started off nervously, Kevin in truth was more concerned with 'how's that physically possible?'

Jane asked about her mother and Kathy spoke to her for a moment, the others listening but more by purposeful accident. "She's always been desperate to have a grandchild before she dies. She cried when I told her and she just lit up. I've never made my mother cry with happiness before."

Kevin pulled a letter from his jacket, "And this is my letter of resignation," he announced. "I'm quitting teaching. My one month notice will start on Monday."

Once again, slightly stunned reactions all round.

"Tom had it in a nut shell. Do what you need to do to make yourself happy, he told me. What makes me happy is writing stories for children, four and five year olds. With the money I had left me when dad died I can afford to take a year off and that's what I'm going to do. And if worst comes to worst I'll go back to teaching, the four and five year olds this time though."

Their congratulations to each other were interrupted by the waitress, Sarah Thomas, a short thin girl they'd been in school with. When she saw their faces she was stunned, shocked and became visibly paler. "Oh my, I didn't expect to see you in here under the circumstances," she said, not too coherently.

"Sarah?" Jane said, "I didn't see you at the reunion last night..."

"I had to work," Sarah replied, half-heartedly.

Jane knew, perhaps to her own shame a little, that Sarah had never been very popular at school. She'd have had to be dragged kicking and screaming to the reunion.

"Circumstances?" Kevin asked.

Once again, Sarah's face was one of shock. "Oh my God you haven't heard. Tom's had an accident. It's in the local rag...hold on." She ran off.

"What's she talking about?" was asked a few times before she reappeared with the local 'Record' newspaper, which had a large photograph on its front page of Tom.

She handed it to Kevin, he read the headline out loud, "'*Local man killed – School Reunion Tragedy*'"

The others gathered round to read:

"Late yesterday afternoon, travelling from home in London to his high school reunion, local man Tom Pearson, age 28, died in what police are calling a freak accident.

It is believed that the driver of a transit van lost control of his vehicle in extremely poor driving conditions. The van crossed the central reservation in to the path of Mr Pearson's car. Emergency services were unable to revive Mr Pearson, who was pronounced dead at the scene... "

"This can't be right, I spoke to him," Kevin argued, shaking visibly. He handed the paper to Adam.

"We all did," Jane agreed.

"I sat in his car while I was waiting for my taxi," Kathy told everyone. "If it wasn't for him I doubt I'd have been able to face my mother at all last night..."

"We'd still be arguing if it wasn't for him," Jane thought out loud, holding Adam's hand.

"It was on the news too, apparently he was quite well known in the advertising business and they even played the advert he did the song for," Sarah told them all. "They showed his picture."

"It's not a mistake," Paul said finally. "They don't make mistakes like this. Not the newspaper and television together."

Shocked, shaken and with some of them moved to tears, very sobering thoughts went silently through all their minds.

THE DISPLACED

I find age a bewildering thing.

Years ago I would have said more so to the young, but now it seems more so to the old. More so to me.

I never quite understood it and don't remember ever being aware of it as it crept upon me. It's a stealthy thing.

I do remember quite a few of my birthdays, even the ones that passed me by without any form of celebration. I suppose that means I was aware of getting older and older and older still. I didn't feel twice as pissed off at 60 as I did at 30: that was a good thing I suppose.

I remember my grandmother saying, 'old age doesn't come alone'. Well she was right enough, for that matter middle age didn't come alone either, but that's another matter altogether.

Of the things old age does bring with it. There seem to be so many. The creaking bones that I heard as a lad when my grandparents got up out of their chairs, the slowing down of your stride as you walk and the inevitable leaning on a walking stick as you start that old-persons stoop. I never got to a point where I needed a walking frame, or 'zimmer frame' as we used to call them when I was younger. I used to find the idea of 'zimmer frames' quite funny back then. Quite a while ago now of course.

Your eyes start to weaken, as does your bladder. Your bowels forget to be regular and when you're listening to someone you find yourself leaning ever so slightly towards them to hear them better. A few years later you're attending a fitting session for a hearing aid.

When I was younger I never seemed to need too much sleep. That was one of the few things I did notice creeping upon me. I spent most of my life with a certain routine. Bed before midnight, up at 7am. Gradually that changed. I started to go to bed a little earlier so as to be able to get up at my normal hour. As I reached retirement I slowly realised that there was nothing to get up for and that an extra hour in bed was a luxury I could now enjoy after a lifetime of getting up early for work, 8am became 8:30am, which soon became 9am and from there it became 'I'll get up when I feel like it'. Early if there was something I wanted to do or somewhere I wanted to go, late if I wanted to enjoy the warm quiet comfort of my bed.

I do find myself thinking of some strange things as I stand here. I think it's the mountain that does it. As I look towards what I think is south-ish, at that lump, I always find myself thinking of strange things. Indeed, the mountain itself, there's an example. That mountain grabs my attention every time, 'Blorenge'. What a weird name for a mountain. Sounds like a dessert gone wrong. But that's the name it's had for more time than I'd care to count. From here it seems quite ominous, almost as if it's a phenomenal landslide just waiting to happen. It seems unbalanced almost, towering over me so.

I see they've completed the road at last. And about time. That was a death trap for so long and now they've duelled it. It's taken years and who knows how many lives. Let's hope it saves a few now.

The scenery is good today. Moody. Not a sunny picturesque day but one with character.

I seem to come here often but never tire of the place, mind you, not as often as I used to. I used to have to come here a couple of days a week when I worked for the local council - 'worked' and 'council' being two words forever linked by the common sound of laughter in my mind.

It seems that there are often little changes these days, just little things I notice from visit to visit. There are always things to see. Not so long ago they demolished the old loo and installed a new one, quite tidy too. You know, I had been coming here for years off and on but it was only when I was working here and had to service the thing that I found there was a loo here. Why the hell do you need a loo up here? I mean, who's going to use it?

At least the people who are doing my old job now are doing a decent job. I used to take pride in my hedgerows. Anyone can cut grass, pick up litter and so on. Hedge trimming, these little hedges, less than a foot tall, they're not so easy to tend. One badly aimed slice with the cutter and the whole thing's ruined. Ruined for now and for months to come. I only made that mistake once. After that I was very careful, proud and successful in tending hundreds of metres of the stuff. It was actually commented upon once or twice by the supervisors when they made their rounds. After a while they became solely my responsibility.

The wind is strong today. I always remember the wind being strong up here. Even in the hottest of summers, if there were any wind at all, it would seem abnormally strong up here. The number of people I've seen up here running around chasing hats, scarves, papers... I must admit that that is one of the strangest things for me to be missing right now: the feel of a strong wind biting into me. Most people know they should wrap up warm when they come up here.

The clouds are thickening up, I can see there have been a few other people up here today but it's quiet right now. That's the best way. I used to enjoy it being a bit busy when I come here. It always seemed better somehow when there were people around, but when you're ignored - it's far better to be alone altogether.

It can be a soul-destroying experience, being surrounded by people and yet still being so totally alone. Not pleasant at all.

The ground is quite firm looking, probably hasn't had any rain for a while... A rarity up here. Doesn't look as if it'll last though, not by the look of that sky.

Time to move I suppose.

No visit would be right without walking my normal route, so I should make a start. I used to amble a bit. But I seem to lose my bearings if I go too far. Finding my way back to where I started becomes a problem...

Oh now that is good news. They've finally had the sense and the decency to close the allotments. I always thought that was in very poor taste having a group of allotments at the base of this incline. Separating the two areas with a flimsy fence. All the goodness in the ground may indeed make for great potatoes but let's be frank here. Where's the goodness coming from?

It's all looking a bit of a mess. But I'm sure it'll be tidied up. They're usually good at that sort of thing. I'm so glad they've seen sense at last, I actually voiced my concerns on that years ago. Wasn't listened to of course. Oh, now that's made my day.

Anyway, to my usual rounds... Checking in on the people departed that I knew and the two whom I helped put at rest when I worked here. Oh, those were strange days indeed.

Try to imagine it. You're a quiet man, working hard, doing his job well and keeping his head down. Respectful of the place where you've been entrusted to work and one day you're told that the sexton needs help with the digging... And later he needs help with the filling in. I will never forget the bizarre all-sensory tingling sensation of shovelling dirt - and I stress, shovelling by hand - onto a box encasing a person's mortal remains. No one should ever have to experience the awesome sense of finality that that carries with it. You feel as if you are standing at the doorway of death, peering over the threshold to the sacred abode of the departed, at one of the new inhabitants.

It gave me a far greater respect for the place I can tell you. Not that I didn't already have a healthy respect for it before. But from that day the stakes were higher. The perception more acute.

YOU try spending up to eight hours a day working in a cemetery.

I can assure you that your mind does make some quite erratic jumps. The people around you could be forgiven for thinking you were on something some of the time.

After two more years of it I had to give it up. I was lucky. I got a transfer almost as soon as I asked for it.

As I look around the place now, quiet, calm, well-tended I think back to those days...they were good days. At the time they were odd, full of hard work, early mornings and the occasional trainee who thought that this place was the best job imaginable...like working in a hotel where none of the guests could complain. In reality they were perhaps the best days of my life, but I do find myself thinking that I missed perhaps the biggest lesson. That perhaps I just didn't get the point of it at all.

It didn't register in my head, not for one single minute of all the time I was working here, that one day I myself would be a resident.

Well now I am.

And I walk a circuit occasionally. Totally alone.

I attend the odd burial: no one ever sees me.

In the early days I would find myself trying to talk to or console the mourners. But I remain as I have been for years now, unseen and unheard. Now and again I actually see a mourner that I knew in life. Being unseen and unheard can be so hard then.

My own grave has a stone, but never any flowers.

My grass gets cut regularly and every time the guy tends me I thank him in unheard words. Perhaps one day, in some way he will know my thanks.

I have been here for a few years, now. I will be here for 100's of years to come, maybe more. But that is just the first few moments of the dawn of eternity. Right?

My lot isn't a bad one.

I can't believe that all the inhabitants of this place walk unseen and unheard, even by the others that share the place.

So I prefer to think that in death, as in life, I have been entrusted with keeping an eye on the place.

That is my lot.

Printed in Great Britain
by Amazon.co.uk, Ltd.,
Marston Gate.